ILK
DET

IN THE BLOOD

Lydia Ackland was nearly blind when she fell downstairs and was killed. Her grandchildren have always accepted the official verdict—accident. Besides, they have their own problems: beautiful Kate is ending a love-affair; her brother Daniel is painfully crippled.

But then that letter comes to light. Only days before her death, somebody wrote and warned their grandmother that she was 'opening a disastrous Pandora's Box' and should 'let sleeping, and perhaps dangerous, dogs lie'. The letter goads Kate and Daniel into asking lots of questions.

First, who wrote it? And why does the answer, once discovered, point to their arrogant Uncle Mark, who, with his ambitious wife Helen, has inherited Longwater, the vast family estate, and the vast fortune that goes with it.

Why were Mark and Helen banished from England in their youth, and what are the secrets behind their long European exile? Kate follows their footsteps through Italy and Corsica, while Daniel continues to ask questions in England. Within days, both their lives have been threatened, confirming their suspicions that all is not as it seems—and perhaps never has been . . .

BY THE SAME AUTHOR

DAY OF THE ARROW
W.I.L. ONE TO CURTIS
THE DEAD MEN OF SESTOS
A MAFIA KISS
PHOTOGRAPHS HAVE BEEN SENT TO YOUR WIFE
VOICES IN AN EMPTY ROOM
ASK THE RATTLESNAKE
LION'S RANSOM
SEA CHANGE
DEATH WISHES
LOADED QUESTIONS
LAST SHOT
CRACKPOT

IN THE BLOOD

Philip Loraine

Collins Crime
An imprint of HarperCollins*Publishers*
77–85 Fulham Palace Road, London W6 8JB

First published in Great Britain
in 1994 by Collins Crime

1 3 5 7 9 8 6 4 2

© Philip Loraine 1994

Philip Loraine asserts the moral right to be
identified as the author of this work.

A catalogue record for this book is
available from the British Library

ISBN 0 00 232506 3

Text set in Baskerville

Photoset by Rowland Phototypesetting Ltd
Bury St Edmunds, Suffolk
Printed and bound in Great Britain by
HarperCollins Book Manufacturing, Glasgow

All rights reserved. No part of this publication may be
reproduced, stored in a retrieval system, or transmitted,
in any form or means, electronic, mechanical,
photocopying, recording or otherwise, without the prior
permission of the publishers.

CHAPTER 1

It wasn't surprising that various objects had slipped down the gap at the back of the shelf and so into the cavity between the wainscotting, on top of which the shelf rested, and the wall behind it. This wall was damp, the panelling had warped, causing the gap to grow wider over the years; hence the arrival of Kevin and Ted from J. Frawley & Son, Builders; hence clouds of plaster dust and the splintering of rotten pine.

'Ho,' said Kevin, 'got some treasure trove here,' and he produced from behind the skirting-board a turquoise-blue comb with several teeth missing, a rusted pair of nail-scissors, two pencils, half a ballpoint pen, the china lid of a Gentleman's Relish pot, several safety-pins, a tangle of string and a handful of pieces of paper: bills, shopping lists, a picture postcard of Notre Dame, envelopes and a letter or two: the detritus of years, laced with dusty spiders' webs. The shelf, just by the kitchen door, had always been a good place for putting things so that you'd know where they were.

Kate Ackland took an old tray from the rack and piled the 'treasure' on to it. Her brother, Daniel, supported by his crutches and the wall, said, 'That one on top, that's Grandmother's writing.' Since the grandmother in question had lived here at Woodman's for several years this wasn't surprising. Kate took the tray into the living-room and put it on the table, thinking how strange it was that after so long she could still be amazed at the dexterity of her crippled brother's movements; he swung himself from his crutches into the wheelchair with an economy of effort which was almost graceful, at the same time propping the crutches against the wall where he could reach them with ease.

She left him examining the contents of the tray, and returned to the kitchen to make tea for Kevin and Tom. Both young men eyed her with appreciation; both would probably have said that she was beautiful, but Kate knew she was nothing of the sort, or only at certain moments in certain lights. She knew she had good eyes, clear grey-blue, good skin, good hair and, thank God, a good slim figure; but, as she'd learned with some surprise over the years, these attributes were all subject to one other mysterious element: her personality was 'attractive', not only to young builders but to almost everybody—male or female—who encountered it. She accepted this as an endowment of providence, not even realizing how much of it was due to the fact that she liked people; was genuinely interested in what they had to say, gave them her whole attention.

Tea dispensed, she went back to the living-room and found Daniel, reading glasses on the end of his nose, examining what looked like a letter. She said, 'Nothing really interesting, I bet—there never is.'

Daniel waved a sheet of creamy, damp-blotched paper. 'This is interesting. Weird really.' He pushed it across the table towards her.

My dear Lydia,

I've asked Sally to read you this letter, and I've explained to her that it concerns a very private conversation you and I had last Saturday evening. (I must add, in passing, that you couldn't possibly have found a nicer, more tactful and loyal companion and/or pair of eyes.)

Lydia, don't be angry with me, but I really do feel that somewhere, deep in the subconscious perhaps, this bee in your bonnet is connected with Richard's death. Yes, I know it happened ten years ago, but you loved him so very, very much and, whatever some people say, one doesn't 'get over' the loss of a beloved son, particularly under such sudden and shocking circumstances.

The other night you called me a coward. I know I've never been as strong-minded as you, but I *absolutely* believe that in this case I'm talking sense. Whether you're right or wrong will make very little difference now; either way you'd be opening a *disastrous* Pandora's Box, and either way people will just dismiss you as a 'batty old woman'. Because the fact is, we *are* both old and one does tend to imagine things.

By now I've probably irritated you quite enough, but I must repeat what I said when we parted. If you do decide to take steps, *for God's sake* talk to Andrew first. I know he's a bore, like most lawyers, but he hasn't known you for fifty years like old Godfrey, so his advice would at least be unbiased, and perhaps he can convince you to let sleeping (*and perhaps dangerous*) dogs lie.

Lastly, Lydia my dear, I must confess how sorry I am that I lost my temper when you said it was all in the blood—and I certainly shouldn't have used the word 'snobbish'. I was overwrought and so desperately worried about your state of mind.

I've asked Sally to burn this when she's read it to you.
God bless you, my dear,
as ever yours . . .

The signature was not only an illegible scrawl but a brown stain of damp ran across the middle of it; moreover, the writer had put neither a date nor her address at the top of the page.

Brother and sister regarded each other in silence with identical eyes. Daniel's hair was also the exact glossy brown of Kate's; he was two years younger than his sibling, twenty-one, and like her, good-looking, though in his case the looks were pinched and hollowed by the years of pain he'd suffered because of his legs. She would not at the moment consider his legs, she spent too much of her time worrying about them. Besides, they were both disturbed by the letter which had so much of the past, of their own selves, contained in it.

The Lydia to whom it was written had been their paternal grandmother, and the Richard whom she had loved so very very much had been their own father; moreover his death 'under such sudden and shocking circumstances' had been caused by the same car crash which had crippled his eight-year-old son. Kate, in the back seat, had survived unhurt, and their mother happened to have stayed at home that afternoon, making curtains. Twelve, no thirteen years ago. If Kate closed her eyes she could see, in the most exact detail, the blue BMW crumpled against the concrete buttress of the flyover, firemen, ambulance crews, police at work around it, the line of crawling cars from which shocked or merely curious faces contemplated disaster, the angered policeman who was urging them to get a move on. It had been one of those hot white summer days, the trees almost black against a glaring sky: somewhere the distant grumble of combine harvesters. Luckily the car had not caught fire or they would never, they later said, have been able to cut Daniel out of it alive.

Brother and sister knew that they were sharing, insofar as they could, the same thoughts and memories; they always knew when this was so. Daniel tore them both away by saying, 'What do you suppose the bee in her bonnet was on that occasion?'

'God knows! She always had one.' No need to add that they were often eccentric or unreasonable. For instance, she had never really forgiven her grandson and granddaughter for surviving the crash when her darling Richard had not. She knew how unfair this was, being neither stupid nor bigoted, but, as obviously, whenever she thought of them or—worse—whenever her cool grey eyes came to rest on them, she could not stem the surge of anger and grief. In fact, it was some years before she could bring herself to speak to them at all. As for their mother, the widow, Lydia had considered her eventual remarriage to be outright betrayal, even though it came five years after Richard's death; but then she had naturally never liked her daughter-in-law in the first place.

Daniel said, 'I'd almost forgotten Sally.'

'We only met her two or three times.'

'She was marvellous with grandmother, I don't know how she stuck it.'

'I think she quite loved her in a funny kind of way.'

'I wonder what became of her.'

Kate considered possibilities and replied, 'Well, if she's not married, men must be stupider than I thought.'

Daniel pulled the letter to his side of the table and stared at it, frowning. '"A disastrous Pandora's Box"! She must have got her teeth into something *really* nasty. Who's this lawyer called Andrew?'

'No idea.'

'I suppose Sally put the letter on that useless shelf, and then drove herself around the bend looking for it, wanting to burn it as instructed.' He peered at the bottom of the page. 'Looks like an R, doesn't it? Rosamund?'

'We're not likely to know, Daniel, we never . . . really entered into her life, did we?'

'No date either.' He sounded disapproving. 'Just what you'd expect of a woman who thinks all lawyers are bores!' His work, at which he was expert, was research, legal and to a lesser degree historical; dates mattered to him. The university had started him off in this capacity when yet another operation had put paid to his chances of a degree in Law. Research meant frequent visits to various libraries which he managed in a specially converted Mini with automatic transmission; his right leg could operate the pedals ... but for how long? Only last week the specialist had told Kate that the leg was deteriorating; she had already sensed this; Daniel made no mention of it, naturally. His bravery, the sight of his brown head bent over the letter, and his glasses sliding down his nose as usual, brought tears to her eyes, tears of pity and of anger—she loved him so very dearly.

Brushing away any sign of emotion with the back of her hand, and pretending the movement was really made to stifle a yawn (he couldn't bear to be pitied) she found herself wondering whether this all-absorbing love for him tended to unbalance her feeling for other men. Recent events indicated that it might be the case; she had become embroiled in the kind of emotional trouble for which previous experience had, very evidently, failed to prepare her.

She was relieved to be jolted out of these thoughts by Daniel saying, 'Hey, wait a minute!' The semi-trained legal mind had come to life. 'I wonder if the *envelope's* here.' He spread out the mess of old bills and shopping lists, and found a matching crumple of cream-coloured paper. 'Yes. Same writing.' He smoothed it out carefully and held it nearer to the window. 'By God, you can actually read the postmark for once. Salisbury. Can you think of an R who lived in Salisbury?'

'No. Is the date legible?'

'Quite recent. 1990.' He leaned towards the lights, gave the wheelchair a twist and moved a yard forward. 'November 1990, can't see the actual date, it's smudged.'

Kate said, 'She *died* in November 1990.'

'That's right.'

'So this must have been about the last bee she ever had in her bonnet. Poor old Gran!' As always the thought of Lydia's death made her glance towards the staircase which clung to the further wall of the living-room. She stood up and went to look at it. Since their grandmother's day an electric chair-lift had been installed for Daniel's use—press a button and it made a purring ascent or descent, sliding on a rail.

'If this had been there then she'd never have fallen.'

'You think she'd have *used* it!' Daniel took off his reading glasses and leaned back, smiling.

'No, she probably wouldn't.'

'I'm damn sure she wouldn't. She was an independent, bloody-minded old woman.'

Kate nodded. There were redeeming features, but in the years following her favourite son's death the description was by and large fair. 'You do take care, don't you, Daniel?'

'Care! I rise into heaven like Apollo in some eighteenth-century opera.'

'No, I mean at the top, with your crutches.' She had never been able to erase from her mind the irrationality of her grandmother's death. 'Why the hell didn't she call for Sally if she felt . . . shaky?'

'Oh, come on, you know she wouldn't! She'd want to prove she could still do it on her own, shaky or not.'

Kate turned an abstracted gaze on him. 'Just the sort of thing *you'd* do.'

'Kate, I am not going to fall, I don't want to.'

'You think she wanted to?'

'I don't think she gave a damn, not after Father died. She more or less told me so.'

'Told *you!* You were only a child.'

'That made no difference. You don't seem to have understood her at all; she didn't mind being cruel.'

Kate nodded uncertainly. 'She shouldn't have said things like that to you.'

'But that was the point. Since his death she was crippled mentally and I was crippled physically. She was telling me that we were neither of us duty-bound to cling to life if it became impossible.'

Kate was shocked; also touched at how easily he seemed to have accepted old Lydia's parallel which struck her as lopsided, perhaps immoral. He added, 'I was rather impressed—grateful in a way. She never used to treat me as a child; I'm surprised you didn't notice.'

'I suppose I did. She treated *me* like a child, she treated you like Father.'

'Without the love.' He could say it quite uncritically. Sometimes he made Kate feel young and inexperienced, which, in a way and compared with him, she was.

She went back into the room and sat on the sofa. From the kitchen came continued sounds of splintering wood and falling plaster. Kate kicked off her shoes and put her feet up. Daniel asked, 'How's the hotel, how's Alex?'

'Making money, mostly in the restaurant—his cooking gets better and better. He wants me to marry him.' She had worked at Hill Manor for seven years now, ever since, at sixteen, she had decided against higher education in favour of earning money. Any academic talent in the family seemed to have been allocated to her brother: the only thing at which she excelled was languages. This may have had something to do with her finding a good job so easily. She'd answered an ad in *The Lady* and, a week later, been interviewed by Alex and Rosie Stratton at their already successful country hotel. He was then thirty-four and Rosie thirty-seven, wedded less to him than to the gin bottle: plump, lazy, good-natured even in her cups.

From the start, beaming, she had said, 'Better watch it, Katie, Alex has got his eye on you.' Whether this was true or not—and at sixteen it had seemed to her unlikely—she made very sure that neither he nor his wife would ever regret having engaged her. She worked hard, for long hours, and exerted all her charm on their behalf. But Rosie had been right: from his first sight of her, Alex had fallen in love, quietly and gently as he did everything else.

Within three years Rosie had relinquished all responsibility to this level-headed nineteen-year-old, and a year after that she left Hill Manor with relief and forever, going to live with her sister in Torquay, where they both drank gin, played bridge, and behaved like tipsy merry widows. She'd give Alex a divorce, she said, any time he wanted one. He wanted one now; he wanted to marry Kate, eighteen years his junior.

If her brother was surprised by this information he didn't show it. 'What did you say?'

'I said it was a bit of a shock.'

'Which it wasn't.'

'Right. I said I didn't think I wanted to get married just yet.'

'I suppose,' said her brother judicially, 'you could do worse.'

'Of course I could. But I'm twenty-three.'

'And he's fortyish.'

'I don't care about his age.' But even at that moment, thinking of Alex, there flared across her mind the picture of a very different man: young, flushed, black hair falling forward, black eyes glittering as he knelt above her, naked. Steve—one of her less favourite names, but what the hell had that got to do with it? And *he* didn't want to get married either, he'd made that quite clear.

She sighed, thinking that probably the most extraordinary part of it was that it hadn't happened to her sooner. Carefully she said, 'As a matter of fact I've . . . sort of fallen for another guy.'

'Poor old Alex! What's he like?'

'Sexy.' She shook her head violently so that her fine brown hair flew wildly and she had to push it away from her face. 'Oh God, I don't *know* what he's like. Appalling probably.' She had postponed discussing this with her brother for four weeks now; it seemed unkind, even indecent, in view of the fact that he himself was forever denied any kind of sexual fulfilment; yet she had always discussed everything with him. She was touched when he jumped the hurdle for her, as he so often did: '"The ruling passion, be it what it will, the ruling passion conquers reason still."' These occasional quotations seemed to slip into his mind unlearned and unbidden: something to do with his habits of analysis and note-taking. Kate was always astonished. 'Who's that?'

'Pope, I think.'

'Puts it in a nutshell.'

'He usually does.'

'His name's Stephen Callender, he calls himself Steve, he's twenty-eight, he was born in Hounslow, he's sales director for Boyd Electronics.'

'Young to be a director of anything.'

'And our meeting stepped out of the pages of *True Romance*.'

Daniel laughed.

She'd seen him coming into the dining-room, alone but sure of himself, and had moved forward, as usual, to escort him to a table. As soon as he sat down he looked up at her and their eyes met. Something peculiar and hitherto unknown took place in her stomach. She gave him the menu and beat a hasty retreat. But, as in *True Romance*, there *was* no unqualified retreat short of walking away from Hill Manor there and then. When she took him his wine—a good one—he watched her opening it and nodded at her proficiency; then said, 'Can we meet for a drink later, in the bar?'

Naturally, she could have said 'No,' but her heart was pounding in an alarming manner and she felt an overwhelming desire to touch his black hair; she had no control whatsoever over her reply: 'I can't see why not.'

She was sure that Alex would see them together in the bar; if he did, he would immediately sense that the situation was abnormal: Kate alone with a good-looking young man. She had very occasionally been known to join one or two of the old regulars, but only for an anniversary perhaps, or for a birthday celebration: once or twice because they were so rich or famous that refusal would have been professionally undiplomatic. And of course, Alex did see them, and the expression on his pleasant, fastidious face told her that he understood her better than she understood herself.

Meanwhile, as if it was the most usual thing in the world, Steve rested a firm dry hand on her leg under the table, and she, after a moment's witless hesitation, put her own on top of it; their fingers intertwined; the attraction between them was like a powerful spring pulling navel to navel. To Kate it was all bizarre, the more so because it seemed so natural. Well, for God's sake, it *was* natural; and when they eventually found themselves in bed together she realized, as most women do if they ever encounter it, that until this moment she had known nothing about sex, either as airborne ecstasy or remorseless quagmire.

Later, peering at her in half-darkness, he said, 'Have you got a thing going with the boss?'

'No. But he's in love with me.'

'Figures.' And, frowning: 'You'll probably think this is bullshit, but I've never . . . felt quite like this before.'

She did think it was bullshit, but she didn't care. To her brother she said, 'It's hopeless, I've just . . . gone overboard.'

'Had to happen, didn't it?' He leaned forward and, at his most gentle, added, 'Katie, you're a smashing girl. Don't think I expect to have you all to myself forever.'

The gentleness struck her like a blow in the face,

knocking all thought of Steve right out of her mind. She flared up in sudden Kate-like anger: 'What the hell are you talking about. No one, absolutely no one, *ever*, will make any difference to *us*!' In anger she looked for a moment quite beautiful, which seemed to her brother to make the words even less believable. People who have been ill and in pain for a long time possess enormous reservoirs of patience and resignation upon which they can draw at any time; he was amused but not surprised that his sister didn't yet realize this. Grandmother Lydia had realized it all right, because she shared it; that was why she had treated him as a grown man, even when he was fourteen.

As so often, Kate was aware of what was in his mind; her eyes strayed back to the staircase. She said, 'We weren't all that interested, were we? I mean, we heard that she'd fallen downstairs and killed herself, we didn't *do* anything about it.'

'She was never very nice to us, not after Father died. And anyway, I was in hospital yet again, you were virtually running a busy hotel, and Mother was married to Colonel Alistair in Aberdeen.'

'She was always beastly to Mother.'

'Always.'

'We didn't even come down for the funeral.'

'I'm not sure we were asked.'

'I hate funerals anyway, but that's not the point. *How* did it happen, Daniel? And *why* wasn't Sally around? Suddenly I want to know.'

'Then pop up to the big house and ask The Cousins, they've probably got all the answers.'

'The Cousins' was their generic term, dating from childhood, not only for Giles, Lucy and Miranda Ackland who were in fact their first cousins, but also for Uncle Mark Ackland and Aunt Helen Ackland, his wife. The appellation had gained considerably in meaning when Kate and Daniel had come to read John le Carré and could appreciate the subtle, faintly derogatory manner in which, according to that writer, British Intelligence referred to American Intelligence as 'The Cousins'. It exactly fitted their own uneasy relationship with the rest of their family.

In answer to her brother's suggestion, Kate replied, 'I don't want to ask The Cousins.'

'Ditto.'

'I don't even want to *see* The Cousins.'

'Ditto.'

And, in unison: 'The Cousins are *rat-shit*. Amen.'

It was the old childhood litany, and still, so many years later, it made them both laugh.

CHAPTER 2

In her ignorance of passion—that unbroken maverick which can confound even the most cold-hearted—Kate was irritated to find that she could lie in bed, sleepless, her mind filled with one single and overwhelming desire: to feel Steve's nakedness against her own.

After a time, a long time, she found that she could exorcise him by fixing her mind on another persistent dilemma: that strange letter. What bee in her grandmother's bonnet could have produced so agonized, even panic-stricken a reaction from the unknown R of Salisbury? 'You'd be opening a *disastrous* Pandora's Box . . . If you do decide to take steps, *for God's sake* talk to Andrew first . . . perhaps he can convince you to let sleeping (and perhaps dangerous) dogs lie.' And why had the writer thought it necessary to ask Sally to burn the letter? It said nothing specific, was in fact maddeningly indefinite.

As for Daniel, he'd been teasing her when he'd said that if

she wanted to know the answers to any mystifying questions concerning Lydia Ackland she had only to ask The Cousins. He knew as well as she did that old Lydia had never been on anything approaching good or intimate terms with her elder son, Mark—quite the reverse. Kate was vague as to the details; her parents had probably discussed them, but she had been ten at the time of her father's death, and the antagonisms between the two brothers and, particularly, those between their mother and Mark would have fallen into the *pas devant les enfants* department; all the same, she'd gathered that the relationship had always been uncomfortable and could at times rise to savagery. No, there'd be no answers from The Cousins, even if she'd felt like asking any questions; and she didn't.

Thinking about her family—as an antidote to Steve who had come bounding into her life with a flash of lightning like something out of pantomime—she realized that in fact she knew very little. If Grandmother Lydia had doted on her younger son, Kate's father, and hadn't a good word to say for his elder brother, surely this meant that Mark, in his youth, must have behaved very badly indeed. Now, on consideration, it seemed more than possible that this behaviour had led to his departure from England, a long time before Kate herself was born. Had he gone into voluntary exile, or had his mother and father brought pressure to bear on a black sheep? Pressure from Grandfather Robert would have been gentle, therefore bearable; pressure from Grandmother Lydia would have been absolute, possibly virulent.

He must have left some time in the late '60s, shortly after his marriage to Helen, and had not come back until the 1980s, by which time his brother had been killed, and his mother (as a direct result of her favourite son's death, Kate had heard it said) was going blind. The banishment, if that's what it was, certainly had nothing to do with his marriage; Helen had been thoroughly 'suitable', coming as she did from one of the grander, if impecunious, families in the south of England.

All this was, to Kate, old old history, made more distant by her ignorance of the facts. What she, like everyone else, knew for certain was that Mark Ackland had now taken possession of his rightful heritage, donning the mantle of wealth and property which seemed to fit him very well. With his wife and children he lived up at Longwater in royal grandeur, for with the big house he had succeeded to the fortune and to the nearly three thousand acres that went with it. Since the estate was not far from Newbury, only fifty or so miles from London and therefore in an area much coveted by the well-heeled commuter, the value of those spreading acres was astronomical. He also owned villages and many farms, he even owned Woodman's, graciously rented to Daniel, his crippled nephew, at a reduced rent. Apparently this was the ultimate extent of any family feeling; the old hostility towards his brother must have cut deep, and indeed, it seemed to have cut off that brother's children from any familiarity whatever.

Oh, The Cousins were polite enough if chance led to some awkward meeting, and once a year before Christmas, Daniel and Kate were invited to a large party: the kind of party rich people are inclined to give for all the rag-tag-and-bobtail they feel bound—but not overly bound—to entertain. Knowing this, brother and sister never accepted. As far as The Cousins were concerned, she worked in some hotel—as a chambermaid for all they knew or cared—while he was crippled and did odd, charitably inspired jobs, and, to top it all, neither of them had any money. *Finis.*

'The Cousins are rat-shit. Amen.' Kate had never been bothered by them and was not bothered now; they had never played any part in her life, a non-situation which, as far as she was concerned, could continue until they all dropped dead. Ah, but how far *was* she concerned? And how far had a certain letter, not at the moment understood, altered the balance of all their relationships . . . ? But she had forgotten the letter, she had forgotten The Cousins, she had even forgotten the demon lover. She was asleep.

Daniel was not asleep. He slept very little: perhaps three or even four hours a night if he was lucky. His legs pained him, but they'd been doing that for nearly two-thirds of his life; he could live with it, he knew how to arrange them to their best advantage. What really worried him now was the knowledge that his right leg, the one they'd eventually been able to reconstruct with such success, was weakening. He didn't want to go back to hospital; hospitals had scared him from the very beginning when he had lain there feeling trapped while groups of men and women had discussed his legs which, due to anaesthetics, could well have belonged to someone else. Since then he had returned five times for further surgery, and had once or twice descended into such deeps of despair that he had seriously considered the cold, practical advice of his grandmother: for different reasons they neither of them had any obligation to cling to life if it became intolerable.

He felt that things would have been very different if he could have stayed at university and taken his degree; then his life would have had a clear-cut purpose, keeping him in touch with the world and with people; moreover the purpose would have been an end in itself, validating his disability. Daniel Ackland, lawyer, could have heaved or wheeled himself about some city, secure in the knowledge that he was of use. Daniel Ackland, part-time researcher, was too aware of his uselessness even to consider a city life with its many mind-saving interests; and so he lived in a delightful cottage in the middle of beautiful woodland where his only links with the world were books, radio not television (by choice), his work, and the loyalty and love of his sister. Without Kate he might well have foundered, and they both knew it.

In a way he had genuinely loved his grandmother, Lydia; her spiky and eccentric ways made sense to him, even as a boy, and he had often found echoes of her in his study of the Law, with which, though she despised it, she shared an outstanding lack of sentimentality. So it was in many ways fitting that the discovery of an old letter, written to her and then lost, was about to release him from the bondage of uselessness.

It was the kind of situation which even she might have found amusing; he had only ever seen her smile at the wry contradictions of life.

Kate's visits to her brother at Woodman's always felt like weekends, but they could never occupy any part of Saturday or Sunday, when Hill Manor was always filled with guests and fully booked for every meal. Only with the arrival of lackadaisical Monday, or sometimes Sunday evening now that she'd trained her assistant, Maureen, could she escape from her commitments. She knew that in many ways she now *was* the Manor; people who wanted to book asked for her by name and expected her to be everywhere at all times. Alex, in his kitchen, was the most vital component but, a shy man, he preferred to remain unseen; it was Kate's efficiency and poise, and in particular her charm, which oiled the mechanism and kept it in smooth running order. So almost every week, and because Alex gave her very special licence, she was able to spend Sunday night, the whole of Monday and part of Tuesday with Daniel.

This particular visit was almost over; would have been entirely over if Daniel had not said at breakfast on Tuesday morning, 'You know that woman who used to clean the place for Grandmother . . . ?'

'Mrs Tyson, wasn't it?'

'Yes. She still lives in the village.'

For Kate this was a minor turning point. An hour ago in her bath she had decided that the whole business of their grandmother's death, and the ambiguous letter which had preceded it, were matters best left alone. Her review of their relationship with The Cousins had only strengthened this decision. The past had been turbulent, often bitter, and was best left to moulder away in other people's memories, since neither she nor Daniel had any personal memory of it at all. The letter had intrigued them, but if damp had not attacked the wainscotting just to the left of the kitchen door they would never have known of its existence, never have been drawn towards the peculiar but irrelevant questions it raised. They had their own lives to lead.

But, she now supposed, there was something more profound lying beneath the calm surface of such reasoning, because her heart jumped at her brother's piece of information and she knew that nothing on God's earth could make her drive away until she'd heard what Mrs Tyson might have to say.

'How would we . . . I mean, she'll think it a bit odd, us suddenly asking questions about things that happened years ago.'

'Why?' He held up the now dry but still stained sheet of creamy writing-paper. 'Why shouldn't we be curious? *She'll remember that shelf.*'

Meg Tyson had not changed at all in the five years since they'd last seen her. She was one of those women, aged perhaps fifty, in whom one could clearly see the girl she had been at fifteen: a tip-tilted nose, a firm mouth not much given to smiling, fairish hair, hardly showing a streak of grey, pulled back into a bun. Kate would have betted that she still put it in pigtails at night.

They joined her for a cup of tea in her small kitchen

where an ancient but immaculate washing-machine grumbled and gushed in the corner. On the other side of the room an old man sat on a window-seat, filling in football-pools with much reference to various tattered sports pages.

'Takes them serious, don't you, Dad?' There was no answer. Mrs Tyson touched her ear by way of explanation. She wasn't at all surprised to hear that a number of things had dropped down the back of the shelf. 'Tried sticking Sellotape along it, I did, but the damp soon put paid to that.'

When it came to somebody whose christian name began with R who lived in Salisbury, who had stayed a weekend with Lydia Ackland shortly before her death, Mrs Tyson was flummoxed, with good reason: 'I used to go up Mondays, Wednesdays and Thursdays, you see. There was that much to do here come weekends.' So any guest arriving on a Friday and leaving on Sunday evening, or even early on Monday, moved in and out of Woodman's with her never having seen them. 'I remember helping Sally make up the spare bed a while before Mrs Ackland's death, but just when . . .' She shook her neat head.

Kate said, 'We thought we might talk to Sally too, but we don't know where to find her.'

'Ah! Well that's something I *can* tell you. Never misses a Christmas, bless her.' She went to a drawer in the dresser. 'Such pretty cards, I can always put a finger on them. There we are, Mrs Ferris she is now.'

She had hitherto shown a commendable lack of curiosity about the contents of the lost-and-found letter, but now, as she put the Christmas card on the table, Kate noticed her taking a good look at it. She and Daniel had decided that they'd be wise to keep its contents to themselves, so she placed Sally's card on top of it and pushed them both over to her brother; he made a note of the address and telephone number, returned the card with a smile, folded the letter and put it in his pocket.

Kate said, 'It's just curiosity on our part.'

'And why not? I can tell you I was pretty curious myself. There was something . . . I don't know, something not quite right about any of that.'

Daniel said, 'You mean her death.'

'Bless you, yes. It wasn't . . . like her to fall, now was it?'

At this, the old man on the window-seat, whose hearing can't have been bad at all, looked up and said, '*Fall!* That's a good'un!'

'Now you be quiet, Dad. Why don't you go down the Woolpack and do them pools there?'

With surprising obedience he stood up immediately, gathering his pieces of paper, and crossed to the open back door. There he paused, looked back at brother and sister, and said, 'Fall my arse!'

Meg Tyson was a trifle—but only a trifle—put out. 'Men! And they call *us* the gossips!'

Both Daniel and Kate had been fascinated by the old man's parting shot. Daniel said, 'Was there . . . you know—a lot of talk about her death in the village?'

'In this village there's a lot of talk if a cat has kittens.'

'But your father,' Daniel persisted, 'seems to think she didn't fall. What's that supposed to mean, that she was pushed?'

'Oh heavens, there wasn't no end to the daft stories went around! But if you said, "All right, who pushed her then, and what did they stand to gain?" they'd scratch their heads and look stupid—and so they are. Then there was a lot of nonsense about thousands of pounds under the floorboards and a fortune in jewellery. I sometimes think you could certify this whole village and do no injustice.'

'All the same,' suggested Kate, 'you just said it yourself—there does seem to have been something not quite right about the way she died.'

Despite her little speech concerning the stupidity of her fellow villagers, Meg Tyson was by nature sensible and cautious; she considered the matter in silence for a moment, clearly wondering whether or not to go any further: which lent added weight to her words when finally she said, 'Put it this way. I must have seen Mrs Ackland come down those stairs dozens—no hundreds—of times since she lost her sight, and never once did she ever falter.' With which she shut her prim little mouth tightly to indicate that enough had been said.

This piece of investigation had taken too long, and Kate, who was always back at the hotel by midday, was now late—which meant driving up and over the Cotswolds faster than she felt to be safe. She was therefore abstracted, and Daniel, sensing it, didn't ask questions or pursue his own reasoning out loud. When they reached Woodman's he rolled swiftly out of the car and upright on to his crutches.

Kate said, 'Sorry! You know what I'm like.'

'It doesn't matter—we can discuss it next week. And don't drive too fast, you're not that late.'

He stood there, watching her go, and, as always, the sight of his slightly twisted figure, diminishing in the rear mirror, then lost to sight, aroused in her the usual pang of pity and admiration and love. Sometimes she dreamed he was cured—or was it a dream of their youth before the crash?—and they were running together over short springy turf, running and laughing.

Hill Manor Hotel could hardly have been more perfectly positioned as far as Kate was concerned: only fifty miles from Woodman's, door to door. Daniel had been right, she wasn't that late, but swung into her parking space in front of the no-nonsense Early Victorian façade with ten minutes to spare. The first thing she saw when she went behind the desk was that Mr Stephen Callender had booked into his usual room, Number 22—there had been no prior arrangement.

All thoughts of her grandmother's death and of the mysterious letter, which had occupied her mind during the drive, were instantly forgotten. Her stomach dropped inside her and she could not, for a good minute, think of even one of the many duties she ought to be performing. The reaction seemed to her too extreme; it offended her sense of efficiency.

He did not emerge for luncheon but, according to Room Service, ordered a smoked salmon omelette, green salad, and a bottle of Pils to be sent up to him. This was unusual, but Kate, going into the dining-room to check tables, didn't altogether mind being rid of his presence which, though undemanding, demanded all her attention. The meal on this sunny Tuesday provided trouble enough, with twice the number of expected guests and everybody, for some reason, wanting Dover Sole. Many had to make do with something else because, as was well known, Alex refused to freeze fish or meat.

But despite such preoccupations, Kate's heart was pounding furiously when, at four o'clock, she tapped lightly on the door of Number 22 and went in. She had expected him to be working, but he was standing at the window staring down into the garden, and even though he was smiling when he turned, some trace of a previous thought, an uneasy thought, still clung to him. Kate ran into his arms and, locked in them, his demanding mouth over hers, fell on to the bed beneath him. They had not seen each other for five days—an eternity.

But sexual satisfaction, however absolute, was one thing, that shadow of unease another. Later, when he was propped on one elbow, gazing down at his hand as it moved gently over her body, she again caught some shadow of it behind his eyes. 'Steve, what's wrong?'

Still caressing her, he said, 'This is.'

She sat up, perturbed, but he pressed her down, leaning on her, hairy chest holding her flat. She said, 'Look—if this is some kind of brush-off I'd rather have it straight. I'll survive—probably.'

He grimaced and shook his head. 'I told you I'd never felt like this before; you didn't believe me.'

'No, I didn't.'

'It's true.' She saw that it well might be. 'I want to be with you, Kate. I want us to spend time together, know each other. I don't go for these . . . hurried sessions.' He glanced at his watch. 'Five past five. Less than an hour and you've got to be on duty.'

She nodded.

'I was free all weekend—wanting you, not knowing what to do with myself. But you were working. Then, on Monday when *you* were free, I had to be in Leeds at a conference.'

She looked away from his troubled eyes.

'And even if I hadn't been in Leeds, there's your brother—don't say anything, of course you have to be with him, poor sod!'

'I can't . . . Steve, I won't give up my job.'

'Why should you? You've worked damned hard to get where you are.' He didn't need to say that the same was true of him, she already knew it. Like her, he had seen no point in further education, and in any case, he came of a humble background and didn't possess the qualifications for university even if he'd wanted to go to one. Also, he had a widowed mother in Hounslow who, in spite of a variety of unskilled and demeaning jobs which he hated her doing, was in reality dependent on him.

All this had been woven into his thoughts as he'd stood at the window waiting for Kate, and the more he considered their relationship the less tenable it seemed. He'd become involved with the one girl among hundreds, thousands, whose life ran counter to his. They were fixed in different orbits, forever sweeping past each other in opposite directions.

Steve Callender had started out as a nothing, a dogsbody in one of the larger advertising firms, but he'd been a bright lad, eager to learn, personable, clever at hiding his ambition from those who would resent it. His rise may have seemed spectacular to others, but to him, with his nose to the grindstone, it seemed exactly what it was: years and years of slogging application. The first time he changed jobs it really did look as if he'd misjudged the upward leap and would fall into the gaping abyss of failure. In the event he'd managed to claw his way upward once more and the gamble had paid off. It had also given him courage when, two years later, the opportunity arose again. Knowing he was too young and inexperienced he'd taken another, even more dangerous leap across the chasm to Boyd Electronics; exerting every iota of charm and audacity at his command, and lying through his teeth, he had managed to heave himself up and over and into an executive position: now *the* executive position.

No, he wasn't going to abandon that for any girl, not even for Kate, and because of it he understood that she wasn't going to abandon her job either; she knew it backwards, she was good at languages, and within a year or two she could jump from the eminence of Hill Manor (highly recommended in every guide he'd ever seen) to almost any job she wanted anywhere in the world.

Studying his face, watching the shadows of his thoughts flitting across it, she realized that after all these weeks she was only now seeing it clearly for the first time. Because he was a successful young man in a cut-throat world she had not, until this moment, really believed that he was as soft and vulnerable under the carapace as any other human being. He wanted to spend time with her, he wanted them to know each other and understand each other as deeply in their hearts as they had, from the first moment, understood each other in their bodies.

It shamed her that he had the courage and honesty to face up to the fatal divergence between them whereas she had not. Somewhere at the back of her mind arose the unwelcome thought that he could do this because he genuinely loved her while she had merely been overcome by lust for him.

She rolled off the bed and went into his bathroom for a shower. Normally he would have joined her and they would have indulged in the usual amorous games; but this time he did not, and she felt bereft, already lost without him.

Enfolded in a vast towel she went back to the bed, where he was still lying, and studied him. Weakly, but then she felt weak, she said, 'I . . . don't think I can take it, Steve.'

'Oh God, how d'you think I feel?'

She would like to have said that she loved him, but had long ago made up her mind never to say it until she was absolutely sure. So she *wasn't* absolutely sure! Looking up at her woebegone expression, he reached out and pulled her into the sitting position, facing him squarely. 'Look,' he said, 'it's really nothing to do with us as people, it's our jobs. We're neither of us going to give them up; why the hell should we? We're not children, we know what life's about. You may want to go on with this . . . hole-and-corner affair, I don't. I care for you too much, Kate, and we're going nowhere.' He echoed it with passion: '*Nowhere!*'

'Do we . . . you know, have to make it final?'

'Jesus, how do I know? What's "final" anyway? But we've got to break the link, we can't go on seeing each other, it'd be too painful.'

'It's painful anyway.'

'Kate.' He took her by both shoulders and shook her a little. 'We must be able to live without this constant . . .'

'Interference?'

'Sounds awful but it'll do. Interference. Always wanting to be with you when it's impossible. I damn near cocked-up an important meeting yesterday.'

Kate stood and moved away, troubled by a suspicion that he might be right. What about the stab of irritation she'd experienced because his unheralded arrival had momentarily undermined her famous efficiency? And hadn't she been relieved not to have him in the dining-room, knowing how much his presence there would have unsettled her? She grimaced at these thoughts and said, 'I tell you what, let's plan to go on holiday together. We really might . . . one day.'

Gently, because she sounded so forlorn, he replied, 'Yes, love, we might.'

'I know it's a bit wet, but I can bear it that way, Steve. It's the finality I can't take.'

'OK. I'll book a couple of weeks in Shangri-La—how about September?'

They smiled tenuously at one another. Only later would Kate wonder if, like her Scottish mother, she was subject to second-sight.

CHAPTER 3

After a restless night—that same ache for a warm body which wasn't there, might never be there again—Kate realized that work would automatically carry her along until mid-afternoon when it was her habit to take a few hours off, either in the garden or with feet up on her bed. She knew the kind of thoughts which would then seize hold of her, and took steps to circumvent them. She rang Daniel. He sounded chirpy, full of energy, but this was a telephone manner he kept for her, and it could mask any kind of pain or despair. She said, 'I've just been looking at the map. Doesn't Sally live in the Vale of Evesham?'

He read out the address: Somerton Farm, Little Norton, near Sedgeberrow.

'It's not far from here—Roman roads most of the way. I think I'll go there this afternoon. Want to drive up and join me?'

No, Daniel didn't think so; he didn't feel much like driving (his way, Kate was sure, of not referring to the useable leg, deteriorating. Dear God!) and he had a lot of stuff to type up for Dr Forrester, some Oxford professor whose book on Cardinal Wolsey he'd been researching. He said, 'You go and see Sally, I'll stick with the old professor.'

'You've still got the letter, haven't you?'

'No. I put it in your glove compartment yesterday.'

'Take care of yourself. Eat properly.'

'Ava's in the kitchen right now, making me a chicken pie.' Ava (three times a week) had been named after the beautiful Ava Gardner whom her father had worshipped. She was a very plain girl, a reasonable cleaner and a less reasonable cook, but she was cheery and fond of Daniel, and that was what really mattered.

The fine spring weather had faded, and the Cotswold Hills in driving rain soon lost their claim to be picturesque and became grim; but as Kate tipped over the edge of them into the Vale, slivers of sunlight lay across the orchards, touching the fruit blossom with delicate promise. Kate hoped Sally's husband was not engaged in that most perilous of businesses—a return of frost had already been forecast. He was not. Somerton Farm had shed its land except for an orchard and the garden, but the barns at its back were in good repair and a few new ones had been added. Ken Ferris was a distributor of agricultural seed and feed and fertilizer.

'Nothing spectacular,' said Sally, 'but safe. Everything has to eat.'

She had always been a big girl; child-bearing and, Kate guessed, uncomplicated contentment had made her bigger: blonde and, yes, voluptuous, with an innocent face, innocent pale blue eyes. In her present state, Kate could and did envy her.

They had tea in an untidy, beamed sitting-room, rambling shambling, toys all over the floor. The two children, one and three years old, were being looked after upstairs by their paternal grandmother. 'With them around,' said Sally, 'we couldn't have got a word in edgewise.' Kate gave her the creamy, blotched sheet of writing-paper. She shook her head over it. 'That damned shelf, I should've guessed. Spent *hours* looking for it. Funny how a thing like this can bring back . . . a whole time of your life. Could've been yesterday.'

'We can't read the signature. We were pretty sure you'd know who wrote it.'

'Mrs Howard, Rosemary Howard. She came to stay that weekend before your grandmother died.'

'From Salisbury?'

'Yes. She lived in The Close, but the house was too big for her, she was selling it.' The pretty face seemed perplexed, blue eyes worried. 'Does it matter?' She was holding up the letter.

'We're just curious. Why do you ask?'

'I don't know.' Perplexity disappeared into a laugh, as it probably always did, she wasn't an introspective type. 'Aren't secrets best left alone? I mean, there's got to be a reason for them *being* secrets in the first place. I always think, "Oh well, it's no concern of mine anyway," but then I'm incredibly lazy—lazy-minded.'

'Curiosity killed the cat.'

'Sort of. Not that I've ever known of a cat killed by curiosity. We've got eleven out in the barns—eleven at the last count, that is. Curious as hell and all *very* much alive.'

Kate said, 'I think Daniel and I are intrigued because ours is a very odd family, full of feuds, hatreds, oh and lots of secrets—they're kind of in the blood.'

Gazing beyond her out of the window, twisting a fair lock of hair, as she probably had since she was a girl, Sally replied, 'My family's as dull as boiled potatoes. She really had it in for her son, Mark, didn't she?'

'Always.'

'I found them a bit . . . weird, him and his wife.'

'They are weird. Pompous too.'

'And living abroad all that time. In Corsica, or was it Italy?'

'Both, I think.'

'I imagined him in Australia, Canada, that's where black sheep usually get sent. Or wasn't he a black sheep?'

'I suppose he must have been. I don't know much more than you do, Sally.' And the purpose of her visit was to ask questions, not to answer them. 'Any idea where this Mrs Howard went when she left Salisbury?'

'She was talking about the south coast, last place *I'd* want to live. One of those stuffy towns, Eastbourne or Bognor. She wanted to be near her son and daughter-in-law—well, she was over eighty. He was a solicitor down there.'

Kate raised her brows. 'Andrew? As in the letter?'

'Yes, of course, Andrew. How dumb of me!'

'She advised Grandmother to talk to him before taking any "steps". I wonder if she did.'

'I know she did; he came over one afternoon. Lots of

curly black hair and very pleased with himself—I thought he was the pits.'

'Even his mother says he's a bore.'

'That too, probably. He just thought he was God's gift. Tried to feel me up in the kitchen, I damn near kicked him in the balls.' She poured more tea. 'Come to think of it, I suppose I was a bit curious about some things . . .'

'Such as?'

'This is going to sound *nosey*, but I never could understand the money side of it. Why did your grandmother have to bury herself away in a tiny cottage? She was used to that enormous house, what's it called?'

'Longwater. She lived there most of her life—until Mark decided to come home and take it over.'

'Why didn't she stay? She could have had a whole *wing*—biggest granny flat in the business.'

'And live with Mark and Helen. You can't share a house with people you dislike, however big it is.'

'No, I suppose not. Is it true he never came back to see her, not once in all those years he was away?'

'Yes, it's true. He might as well have *been* in Australia.' She had realized that Sally was incapable of sticking to one subject for more than a minute. Questions had to be simple and direct: 'So you didn't hear what those two old women were discussing—all that business about opening Pandora's Box, and letting sleeping dogs lie because they could be dangerous?'

'Not a thing. It wasn't my business, and they'd shut themselves up in the sitting-room.' She smiled. 'I do remember Mrs Howard coming into the kitchen and asking me if your grandmother was talking . . . well, a bit wildly—obviously meaning did I think she was getting weak in the head.' She looked at the letter: 'I suppose this bears that out, doesn't it? I said as far as I was concerned Mrs Ackland was as bright as a button. She was—even on the day she died.'

'Must've been quite a shock, her death.'

Sally sat lost in thought, again twisting the lock of hair. Kate noticed that there'd soon be more than one chin, but she probably didn't care. Eventually she said, 'Yes, it was a shock all right, in lots of ways. I mean, *why* was I sent out shopping on that afternoon? For all kinds of things we didn't really need, not urgently anyway. And nothing I could get in the village either, I had to go into town.'

'And when you got back she was dead?'

'Yes.'

'The police must have thought that a bit odd.'

'They didn't seem to. I mean, it tied in with their theory, didn't it? Accident. Blind old lady, steep staircase, companion not on hand to help her.'

With every step Kate took, every odd piece of information that came her way, she realized how little she and Daniel knew about the most basic facts. 'And was that the Coroner's verdict, accident?'

'Yes.'

'No sign of a heart attack or anything?'

'None. That's why a lot of people thought it was suicide.'

'Did you?'

'Good God, no. Why would she want to do that? She wasn't ill or broke, she certainly wasn't round the bend. And anyway a staircase would be such a . . . an uncertain way of doing it. Supposing it didn't come off, you'd end up with a broken leg, hip, you name it.'

'What actually *did* kill her?'

'She hit her head on that ugly great newel-post at the bottom of the stairs. All pointed corners. I'd have sawn it off and chucked it out as soon as I clapped eyes on it.'

They fell silent. Kate had a feeling that there was no more to be learned from this straightforward, uncomplicated young woman; in any case it was time she went back to Hill Manor and got herself ready for the evening. She was just wondering how best to take her leave when, from upstairs, there came a shriek of rage, rising to an ear-splitting crescendo. Placidly, Sally said, 'That's Tom.'

A thudding of footsteps followed, and a moment later the door opened to reveal a small, roly-poly woman of perhaps sixty, only just able to carry a large child, exactly like Sally, and at the moment scarlet with rage. She nodded to Kate and said to her daughter-in-law, 'Sorry, I can't do a thing with him.'

'Little bugger,' observed his mother fondly, taking him in her arms and giving him a massive hug. He stopped screaming instantly. Kate seized the perfect opportunity for escape.

Daniel, when she phoned him that evening, wasn't surprised that Sally had heard nothing of what had been said by their grandmother and her friend. 'If she'd been that kind of person,' he wisely observed, 'old Lydia would never have employed her.' He was much more intrigued by the identity of R, late of Salisbury and now living somewhere on the south coast. 'Rosemary Howard, eh? With a solicitor son, Andrew Howard. You can leave that to me, I'll find them.' And, when Kate expressed doubt: 'Do you mind! I *am* a researcher.'

Like his sister, he thought it odd that Sally had been sent out to do some unnecessary shopping on the afternoon of their grandmother's death. Who or what had Lydia not wanted her to see? Or were more things about to be said which had to be kept secret? In any case, their next move was obvious: they must find Rosemary Howard and they must talk to her—pray God she wasn't dead! There'd be no guessing as far as she was concerned; she *knew*, her letter proved that. What a mercy the terrible shelf had preserved it from being burned by Sally, or they'd have had no reason to embark on this fascinating quest. Contrarily, and only for a split second, Kate found herself wishing that Sally *had* burned it. She was surprised by the wish which had sprung from some inner recess of her mind, almost as if to warn her.

Daniel sensed this. 'What's the matter?'

'Nothing.'

'Suddenly you sounded . . . I don't know—as if you'd gone off the whole thing.'

'Don't be silly, I'm as curious as you are.' She was. And if there were any further reservations lurking in that same recess she could banish them with ease: because there was no mistaking her brother's passionate interest; she hadn't heard him sound so involved for years, and involvement, in his present condition, was worth anything.

Ironically, she was about to surpass him in this respect, propelled by a bizarre series of events, the first being a telephone call from Steve early next morning.

At the sound of his voice her stomach confounded her by turning somersaults, something it no longer had any right to do. He said, 'I'm missing you like hell, Kate.'

'Me, too.'

'So bloody easy to *say* all those pompous things.'

'Yes, but . . . you were right, Steve, we both knew you were right.'

'Sod that too, but we'll soldier on. Look, I'm not calling you just to whinge. What's the name of the disease that's attacking your brother's legs? Raynor's Syndrome?'

'Yes, why?'

'I've got a board-meeting, I'm late. Look at page four of *The Times*, column three. OK?'

'OK.'

'Be in touch.' His receiver was replaced.

Page four of *The Times*, column three, contained a brief

report headed, 'Raynor's Breakthrough'. It appeared that Dr Wesley Allard of the Blake Clinic, Oakland, California, had just released information which seemed to prove that two of his patients suffering from the rare nervous condition known as Raynor's Syndrome were showing signs of total recovery. Treatment had been long and arduous, had included physical and drug therapy, and, in both cases, surgery involving the central nervous system. Though the disease was rare and had hitherto baffled the medical profession, Dr Allard's claim would, if substantiated, bring hope to hundreds of sufferers worldwide.

Astounded, Kate had to read the few paragraphs twice. The news was so unexpected that it shocked her; for a moment or two she felt nothing at all. Then excitement, hope, joy broke over her in a glittering wave; but as the wave withdrew came the instant thought of cost. Useless to pretend that 'long and arduous' treatment at a clinic in California was going to be cheap; but surely there were ways, there *had* to be ways.

She knew she'd be able to think of nothing else all day, and so took the precaution of showing the article to Alex. Though delighted, he tried to warn her of a few of the setbacks and disappointments she might have to face, but Kate was beyond reason, lost in a euphoria of determination and optimism.

After long and agonizing inquiry, she found a telephone number where she could reach the surgeon who had first operated on Daniel and who had returned to the fray three times since then. Yes, he'd heard about the putative cure and was keeping his fingers crossed for Dr Allard whom he knew and liked. But the great difficulty was going to be the matter of cost. Like Alex, he could sense that this overexcited girl had to be seized and bound into the straitjacket of expediency. 'Kate, the Blake Clinic isn't a charitable institution, and it isn't funded by the state. Wesley Allard's research on this project lasted for eight years, and it's got to be paid for.'

'We'll manage somehow, we've got masses of good friends.'

'My dear, will you listen to me? In both the cases cited, treatment lasted about ten months. The Blake charges, say, three-hundred dollars a day, *excluding* any treatment, drugs or therapy, and excluding surgery which was appallingly protracted. We're talking about something well over a third of a million dollars, much more if there are complications, and you'd have to be financially prepared for complications.' He could tell from the silence on the other end of the line that he had at last got through to her.

In a much duller voice she replied, 'But you hear of it all the time. People, children, being sent off for incredibly expensive operations—funded by generous neighbours, all that.'

'And rarely costing a quarter of what this would cost. I'm not trying to put you off, God forbid, I'm only trying to save you a lot of wasted time and heartache.'

She telephoned Daniel's two specialists; and then his National Health doctor in the country. She telephoned various medical men she barely knew (one of them an infrequent guest at Hill Manor) and several more who were complete strangers. She even called the Ministry. Everywhere she met with the same kindness—there was no mistaking her desperate anxiety—and the same warnings. At the end of it, exhausted, she went for a long walk, barely noticing the heavy mist which soaked her.

Alex had money of course, and would probably lend her some, even if it meant postponing a dream cherished for seven years: six new bedrooms and a new kitchen created from the stables. No, she could never ask him. Steve *earned* a lot of money, but had a mother to keep and was desperately trying to save for what he called his 'disaster fund'.

Her mother had a small income of her own which, added to Alistair's army pension, enabled them to live decently, without extravagance, in Aberdeen.

By the time she returned to the hotel, steeled to cope with Friday evening, always a hassle, the idea had entered her mind. By the time she reached Daniel at Woodman's late on Sunday it had possessed her; she knew exactly what she must do.

Her brother, who had long ago heard about Dr Allard's cure, was appalled to find that she had now discovered it: doubly appalled by her proposed solution: 'The *Cousins*! Kate, you *can't*!'

'Watch me.'

'I'd rather . . . Kate, I mean this—I'd rather go on the way I am.'

'Of course you wouldn't.'

'I *would*. Please listen to me. I know it's a . . . a spineless attitude, but I'm . . . used to myself now. It's taken a bit of doing but I've done it. I don't think I could take being in hospital again, for *months*—all that change and confusion. Also, I'm afraid of drugs—you know I am, and I've had enough bloody surgery to last me a lifetime. I'm a coward.'

'That's the last thing you are. You're just scared of the cost like everyone else.'

'Not half as scared as The Cousins are going to be!'

'They wouldn't even notice it, they're *stinking* rich. And I'm not asking for charity, I'm asking for a loan. They'll get it back, every penny. I'm going up to Longwater first thing in the morning.'

Daniel made a face. 'I found out where Rosemary Howard lives—Bournemouth. I hoped we could drive down and see *her* first thing in the morning.' He looked like he had at the age of eight, a disappointed small boy, but she was adamant. 'Later, we'll do that later.' And then, overcome by exhaustion, by what seemed to be the opposition of the entire world, and now by her brother's maddening disinterest: 'Oh, for God's sake, Daniel, this is *important*, it's the most important thing in our whole lives. Finding that letter was just a . . . a crazy chance.'

Daniel nodded; then said, as much to himself as to her, ' "A fool must now and then be right, by chance." Cowper—at least I think it is.'

In her grandfather's day, and even in the years when Lydia had lived there alone—after her husband's death but before the accident which changed her life—the drive at Longwater had always seemed friendly, arousing excited anticipation; now, under the aegis of Mark and Helen Ackland, that same drive had subtly changed its character; though it remained exactly the same, the new intention was simply to impress: curving around the serpentine lake which gave the house its name, crossing the famous Palladian bridge, climbing the hill before plunging into a stand of ancient beeches, and only then granting the arriving guest a first, breathtaking glimpse of the north front with its splendid pillars, classical architrave and all the rest of it. Or perhaps, Kate thought, the change was in her own attitude, and in the difference between childhood and growing up.

Whatever the reason, she had no intention of approaching The Cousins via the enormous front door. This would be opened by their noxious butler, Smart, who would regard her with a disdain which out-cousined The Cousins, making them seem hospitable by comparison. She parked her car in the shade and plunged into a shrubbery to the east of the house, remembered intimately as the scene of countless adventures in Amazonian forests or tiger-haunted Indian jungles, according to the whim of her inventive brother. This way she would approach the garden front, wandering up on to the terrace, and so, unannounced, into their lives. For God's sake, she'd telephoned and made an *appointment*, wasn't that enough?

However, she nearly laughed out loud when she reached the topmost terrace to find The Cousins disposed about the lily-pool as if the curtain had just risen on an old-fashioned West End play. Mark and Helen sat at a white cast-iron table on which reposed a *silver* coffee-pot with accoutrements, including, she noticed, an extra cup for herself. Her uncle had thickened and coarsened since she'd last seen him, and his fairish hair was receding which made his red, admittedly handsome, face seem larger. Her aunt had not changed at all; her dark hair, which never looked dyed, was still arranged in what Kate always thought of as the 'haute-county' style (much in evidence at Hill Manor Hotel): ageless, accentuating an almost ageless neck; and her beautiful face, equally well-preserved, remained youngish, pale, patrician. Both seemed to be designed to decorate the society pages of *Country Life*, or *Queen*, or the *Tatler*—as indeed they frequently had and did. Her beige linen dress was perfection; she invariably wore pearls. All in all, she made her husband, in a brownish kind of safari suit, look lumpen.

It was said that in their youth Mark and Richard had been alike, but Kate felt sure that if her father had lived for another thirteen years he would never have shared the coarsening process which had overtaken his elder brother; he was too neat and slim, and had never been much of a drinker which Mark patently was.

Mother and father seemed to have distanced themselves from the two of their three children who were present. Giles, at twenty, resembled his father and would become as gross; for the moment, his fair, confident good looks gave some indication as to why Mark had always been considered so handsome and attractive. Miranda, the younger daughter, was sixteen, usually an uncertain age and in her case a disastrous one; she was fat and had bad skin, and no one would have guessed she was in any way related to the exquisite woman at the table. Brother and sister both wore tight trousers which, as Giles well knew, emphasized his strong legs and his crotch; whether the girl knew that they merely emphasized her hips and bottom was open to doubt. Lucy, the middle child, now eighteen, had opted out.

This family group was arranged to face away from the house, and Kate was overcome by a wicked certainty that here was a conscious display of backs calculated to greet her with utter indifference. Well she'd certainly scotched that little trick, for now she faced them head-on *and* reflected in the lily-pool. Father and the two children showed surprise, but Helen, in her usual accents of petrified gentility, said, 'Why Kate, how nice to see you, and what a *most* attractive dress!'

Kate suspected that this remark was addressed less to her than to her unattractively-trousered daughter, she was that sort of woman. She and old Lydia together must have made quite a pair!

Mark was meanwhile hrrumphing about, moving chairs and making welcoming noises: 'Don't see nearly enough of you,' and other meaningless pleasantries. Giles, who had at least been expensively educated, stood up and struck an attitude which further enhanced his looks and figure. Miranda waved plump fingers but didn't otherwise move. If either son or daughter imagined they were going to be privy to the ensuing conversation their mother disabused them by saying, 'Giles, you might go to the stable and see what that ass, Kimble, is up to. And take Miranda with you.' Thus do the Helens of this world wave their dainty, razor-sharp wands. Evidently no time was to be wasted in getting down to business.

Telling herself yet again that she was not seeking charity, Kate started by asking whether they'd read in the papers that some Californian doctor appeared to have found a cure for the disease, Raynor's Syndrome, which was ruining Daniel's life.

'Oh,' replied Helen (pronounced 'Eu'), 'we wondered if that's what he's got.' They knew damn well it was, and the pretence gave Kate just that edge of anger needed to liberate eloquence. Yes, she was eloquent, carried away by youth and passionate determination; so that it only dawned on her slowly and painfully that she might just as well have remained mute; have stayed at Woodman's with Daniel, or driven off with him to Bournemouth in search of Rosemary Howard. ('A fool must now and then be right, by chance.' No mistaking the fool in this case: as wrong as could be and without the shadow of a chance.) The Cousins had known from the beginning why she wanted to see them—they were quite used to beggars—and after all it wasn't a great feat of conjecture for a mind like Helen's once she'd read the newspaper; they had long ago decided just how to answer her.

Uncle Mark was first to bat for the Establishment. It seemed that the entire roof, including most of the lead coping, required urgent attention: worse when it came to the east wing where the actual timbers would have to be replaced. A financial disaster of the kind which only struck one if one happened to own a Grade One Listed Property. Somehow this led to the fact that he was responsible for the employment of over two hundred people, and for the direct upkeep of a hundred and seventy-six properties, a proportion of them nothing but almshouses for old employees, bringing in little or no rent. (This, no doubt, included Daniel and Woodman's.) And now, as Kate had probably noticed, the south plantation was dying of some wretched, continental disease, would have to be bulldozed, burnt and replanted . . .

And, added Helen, perhaps fearing her husband might

flag, there was Cortiano. (There was where?) Not an enormous house (pronounced 'hice') with some return from olives and vines. But the outlay was considerable, the place had to be leased—no one in Corsica ever *sold* land—and there were more employees to be paid, taxes . . . Kate had never realized that they'd held on to the Corsican property, perhaps as a nice retreat for secluded holidays.

Now, continued Mark, having regained his breath, if Kate could believe anything so preposterous, the District Council had suddenly announced that the bridge at Little Layton needed rebuilding, and it was his responsibility, nothing to do with them at all.

And then, chimed in Helen again, there was the whole absolutely *fearsome* cost of the children's education, with Giles already at Cambridge and both his sisters proposing to follow in his footsteps. Uncle Mark summed it all up in tones of the deepest despondency: 'They've got us over the barrel, Kate. We're stretched—damn tight. Of course we'd have *leaned over backwards* for a family matter like this, but it isn't feasible, it simply is *not* feasible.'

The humiliation which rose up in Kate, threatening to choke her, had nothing to do with the selfishness and meanness of spirit which lay behind all this verbiage; it had nothing to do with The Cousins at all. The fault lay within herself; that she had ever been so stupid, so childishly optimistic, as to believe that they really might have helped Daniel. God in heaven, anyone would think she knew nothing whatever about the world and its ways! There had never, ever, been the faintest chance of one poor cripple's fate even impinging on their armour-plated indifference: and the hated brother's son at that!

The degrees of growing up are each marked by a milestone. Kate reached one and passed it in triumph by the mere fact of not losing her famous temper: not saying a word of what she really thought, nor betraying her deep contempt in any way. She merely allowed herself to look at each of them in turn, silently, before saying, 'Oh well, it was worth trying. No, don't move, I know this place like the back of my hand—remember?' It was a subtle parting shot, and would leave not the slightest scar, but both faces told her that it hadn't missed its mark.

CHAPTER 4

Kate didn't want to saddle her brother with the bitterness of failure and humiliation, even though he had expected nothing else. She needed to be by herself for a time, and so stopped her car, got out and wandered into the woods, now at the height of their spring beauty: from the gold of the oaks through numberless shades of pale green, doubled and trebled by the play of hesitant sunshine, to the silver of aspen and willow down by the river.

She sat with her back against an ancient beech tree and, looking up into the world it spread above her, saw that two green woodpeckers, early nesters, were already feeding their brood: to and fro, to and fro, caught in the great imperative of nature. She hoped their nest was deep inside the generous grey trunk, safe from marauding squirrels and magpies.

And then, with no conscious change of direction, she found herself thinking of Steve: thinking of him directly, for an awareness of him was always at the back of her mind. She wanted him to be here, leaning beside her against the tree and watching the woodpeckers; and wasn't this what he himself had wanted and could not foresee in their joint future? 'I want us to spend time together, know each other. I don't like these . . . hurried sessions.'

At this moment she could almost believe that she could give up her job and her ambitions in order to be with him, but she was too much of a realist not to understand that failure and humiliation were unworthy fathers to the wish. It seemed strange that she had never told him about her grandmother's letter, and had not seen him since the complications began to multiply around it. If he'd known the facts, how would *he* have reacted to that scene on the terrace at Longwater? With anger on her behalf? No, she thought, with a more subtle determination to get the better of The Cousins; they were the kind of people he'd been fighting all the way from comprehensive school in Hounslow and over a hundred battlefields to his present eminence on the board of directors. He hated them and he knew them, more intimately than Kate herself, despite the fact that in this case they were close relations.

After a while, thinking about Steve and wondering if she would ever stop needing him, and watching the woodpeckers at their mighty labours, the bitterness began to seep out of her as if a blocked drain in her mind had suddenly been cleared. So that when she got back to Woodman's she found herself describing her reception at Longwater House in terms of self-mockery and ironical humour. She knew that her brother, searching her face with thoughtful eyes every bit as shrewd as her own, was not deceived, but her acid description made him laugh and somewhat mitigated the dismal circumstances.

Only now, in more distant retrospect, did she appreciate how childish her appeal must have seemed to Mark and Helen Ackland: as childish as it had seemed to Daniel himself. Once again she faced the fact that even though he was two years her junior he was much older than she was. But her comparative youth had its compensations; she was resilient, her optimism was still intact, and it was strong enough to sustain them both, for her brother had lost most of his during those years of recurring pain, recurring surgery. Perhaps he didn't even realize that behind the mask she had put on for his benefit her determination to get him to the Blake Clinic, to see him cured, had not lost one jot of its urgency, rather the reverse—even if she now had no idea how to proceed.

For the moment she was in limbo, and was therefore perfectly content to drive him to Bournemouth and talk to the old woman who had written that letter.

Rosemary Howard lived to the west of the town near the sandy humps grandiloquently known as Canford Cliffs. The house was large, implying that her residence in Salisbury Close, from which she had moved because it was too big, must have been enormous. With great originality this place was called The Pines, which could as well have described any of the others in Durlston Crescent. All of them sprouted from the omnipresent sand, all were surrounded by pines, and several looked as if they might presently slide, with their trees, down on to the beach. But perhaps they were all safer than they seemed, for most of them had been there for at least seventy years. The Pines was built of painful '20s brick with a wealth of white wooden detail: fretted balconies and eaves and sun-porches, every one surmounted by a finial.

Mrs Howard, they'd been told by a brisk female voice on the telephone, always rested from two until four, but would be delighted to see them at tea-time. The same voice, now issuing from a plain, bosomy nurse, advised them that Mrs Howard was eighty-three and just the tiniest bit vague, she did so hope they wouldn't tire her out, she tired easily. Sometimes she dropped off for ten or fifteen minutes; if that happened, they could either sit there and wait for her to wake up or take a nice walk along the beach.

Thus warned, they were ushered into the presence of a tall, very thin old lady; she sat bolt upright in some kind of orthopaedic chair, examining them acutely with bright blue bird-eyes which gave no impression at all of being 'the tiniest bit vague'. She wore a flowered housecoat, and her head was wrapped in a Hermès scarf fastened with an emerald brooch, either to hide the fact that she had very little hair, or because there'd been no time to tidy it properly.

'My goodness!' she said, 'Lydia's grandchildren, I can hardly believe it!' She must have known all about Daniel's infirmity and made no reference to it, but staring at Kate said, 'You're very like her, you know, when she was a girl.'

They had discussed the wisdom of producing the letter which this old woman had written to their grandmother, but in view of how spry she appeared to be Kate decided to do so; it would prune away whole branches of introductory foliage. Rosemary Howard listened to the description of its chance discovery; then took the discoloured page with faint distaste and examined it through a magnifying glass. Then she was silent for a while, staring out at the English Channel which was in one of its blandly boring moods.

Both Kate and Daniel would have preferred an instant reaction; she was all too obviously considering what she ought or ought not to say. Eventually: 'One's memory fluctuates, you know. I remember writing this, oh, very well. What have you come to ask me?'

'We wondered,' said the forthright Kate, 'just what she said to you in private which . . . made you advise her to keep quiet.'

The old woman looked at the letter again, but did not need to use the magnifying glass, it was really a look into the past. 'If I advised *her* to keep quiet about it, would I discuss it with you?'

'Probably not. It's a risk we decided to take.'

Rosemary Howard nodded with a faint smile. 'You're as blunt as Lydia was.' Then she looked at Daniel, and her expression softened; something about his good looks, coupled with his deformed legs, seemed to have moved her.

'Very odd woman, your grandmother, even if she was an old, old friend—one of my best friends really. Loving your father as much as she did . . .' The voice faded; but she wasn't sliding away from them, so soon, into a nap. 'I can't decide whether it's my memory or whether, that weekend, she really *wasn't* making the best of sense.'

Lydia's grandchildren were both recalling that it was this woman who'd gone into the kitchen to ask Sally if she thought her employer was getting a bit senile; if Sally's contention that she was as bright as a button was true, then Rosemary Howard's memory might indeed be at fault; or she might, for her own good reasons, be pretending it was.

'Well . . . she's dead now, God rest her soul, so I suppose nothing matters greatly any more.' Her tone implied an abandonment of caution, but a sideways glance from the blue eyes seemed to imply something else, something less straightforward. 'It was money she was worrying about.'

'Unlike her,' suggested Kate.

'Not as far as she herself was concerned, not personally. It was all to do with her sons. She had . . . She seemed to have this idea . . . that at some time in the past Mark . . . yes, had cheated her darling Richard.'

'While Father was alive?'

'I think so. She really didn't make any of it very clear. No, not at all. But yes, that was the . . . the gist of it. Mark had cheated your father out of a considerable sum—a very considerable sum. She had . . . only just realized the extent of it, she was very angry.' Both brother and sister could almost feel her mind slipping and sliding around in a morass of half-truths; but half a truth is better than nothing. Kate said, 'If Father was alive at the time, this must have happened when Mark was living abroad.'

'Yes. Italy.'

'Corsica, surely?'

'Italy, Corsica. Yes, it was . . . all to do with that period. As far as I recall. I'm sure you know there was a terrible row over money, years before. He'd been running up debts, staggering debts, and there were . . . other scandals too. Your grandfather found out. That was when they . . . told him to leave England, gave him his marching orders; Helen was furious. Your father was the blue-eyed boy, how Lydia adored him. He went to Italy.'

'Father?'

'No, no—Mark,' with some asperity. 'But things didn't get any better abroad, they seldom do. More scandals, oh dear, yes. He was taken to court by some Italian family, titled, but then they're all titled. That was when your . . . grandparents decided to disinherit him.'

She assimilated their blank, bewildered faces. Daniel said, 'You mean . . . in favour of Father?'

'Who else?' She shrugged. 'Lucky they didn't go through with it, as things turned out, your father dying.'

'This was when they were in Corsica, Mark and Helen?'

'Corsica, Italy, wherever you say. Abroad anyway.'

'Did Grandfather agree with it, the idea of disinheriting Mark?'

'He blew hot and cold. He was always more compassionate than Lydia. But you know how the Acklands feel about Longwater.'

Both Kate and Daniel knew very well. The great house with its enormous domain was their paramount consideration; had been for two centuries. Except for small sums here and there the Ackland fortune (created by pumping-machinery, reinforced by good marriages) was entailed. Whoever inherited Longwater inherited almost all the money, that was the strict tradition. Whatever happened, Longwater must be cherished, must survive unharmed and preferably unchanged. Presumably Lydia and her husband had foreseen that in the hands of their elder son the tradition might well falter, sag, decay. Mark might spend the fortune on riotous living, but the second son, darling Richard, Lydia's favourite, could be relied upon to see that the status quo was maintained. And his son, Daniel, was a sturdy, intelligent child; he had not yet been crippled; he would be trained to carry on. God alone knew whether Mark would sire anything—there had already been one well-publicized 'society' abortion, and no doubt others less newsworthy. Also, the way he lived—and drank—he might kill himself at any moment. Even when he finally married Helen neither of them showed any sign of wishing to produce children.

Kate said, 'Did Uncle Mark ever get to hear about this disinheriting business?'

Daniel, understanding her so well, knew exactly what had flashed across her mind. She already suspected her uncle of evil deeds, and could readily believe that if he heard his younger brother was going to take all, he wasn't above engineering that brother's death in a car crash. A wild, wild idea, but so typically Kate that Daniel had to hide a smile.

'No.' On this at least Rosemary Howard was definite. 'They hadn't made up their minds. I daresay I was the only . . . only person who knew anything about it, and Lydia swore me to silence. They may have discussed it with their boring old lawyer, Godfrey Ashenden, but *he* never talks at all, I often wonder if he's mute.' She closed her eyes for a moment as if to rest them from the two young, demanding faces. Whereas she had at first been sharp and incisive, her speech was now a little blurred.

Daniel said, 'And that weekend, Grandmother was talking about resurrecting this business of the money Mark owed to Father.'

'Did I say . . . ? Yes. Yes, that was it. Most unwise, I told her so. Let sleeping dogs lie, isn't that what I wrote?'

Daniel was wondering why his sister should be looking shocked. The fact was that she had imagined herself to be in limbo and had just realized that limbo didn't exist and never had. There was a line which led directly from Steve's voice on the telephone, alerting her to a possible cure for Daniel, via her defeat on the terrace at Longwater, to this room and this old woman. Because if Mark had really cheated their father, and the fact could be proved (as old Lydia had obviously intended to prove it) then that money would now belong to Daniel: 'a very considerable sum'. Enough to send him to Dr Allard at the Blake Clinic?

She said, 'I don't want to tire you, Mrs Howard, but are you sure of this? Grandmother intended to cause trouble because she'd recently discovered that Mark cheated Father out of a lot of money?'

'Who'd have believed her? Did I . . . Did I just say that, or write it in the letter? Why didn't the girl *burn* the letter?'

'We told you—it fell down behind some panelling.'

'Yes, yes. People would only have said she was a bit gaga, maybe she was. Mark had inherited, and he was making a good job of it. All the past had been forgotten long ago, even that curious *ménage-à-trois*.'

Kate and Daniel both leaned forward as if operated by the same spring. He said, 'What *ménage-à-trois*, Mrs Howard?'

'Oh, long before your time. Are you sure it was Corsica? I thought Italy, I'm sure Lydia mentioned Lasetto or Lazzetta, somewhere like that . . .'

'But,' insisted Kate, 'this *ménage-à-trois*?'

'They were young then, full of all kinds of mischief—well, Mark was always full of mischief. And anyway, it worked out, such things invariably do. They had all those children, they're perfectly happy now, aren't they?' She stared at them for a moment, blue eyes wide, as if she had for a moment forgotten who they were. Then, glancing away: 'Lazzetta, was it? Gerald and I went there once, we loved Italy, particularly Liguria. Utterly spoiled, I believe, and Alassio crawling with Germans.' She shook her head and raised one blotched hand to her cheek. 'Oh dear, have I said too much? It hardly matters, does it? I told her, "Lydia, all this happened *ages* ago. You haven't even got proof. You can't start saying things like that without proof, you'd be making a fool of yourself. Let sleeping dogs lie," I said. I know I was . . . right.'

Her head fell back against the chair. She closed her eyes; then opened them again. 'No, perhaps it was Lasetto. Gerald and I . . .' Then she was fast asleep.

Kate and Daniel went out of a French window, down wooden steps leading from an over-ornate verandah into a sandy garden. Among the pine trees was a white bench, angled so as to give a view of the wrinkled sea, too weary even to produce a proper wave; it also gave a shadowed view of Rosemary Howard asleep. They sat on it.

Kate said, 'You don't suppose old Lydia *was* pushed down those stairs.'

'You mean, by Mark?'

'Yes.'

'Because she was threatening to reveal some ancient story about how he'd once cheated Father out of money?'

Kate had to shrug; it sounded unlikely.

'It wasn't as if there was any secret, Kate. Mark was always cheating people out of money, it was his favourite sport when he was young. He'd hardly kill his own mother for talking about something which had been common knowledge for thirty years!'

'In that case Rosemary Howard's over-reacting, isn't she?'

'Looks like it. Mind you, it would have been *awkward* of Grandmother to go digging up the past—awkward and bloody-minded.'

'Which she often was.'

'Sure. But Mark would have ignored the whole thing, wouldn't he? And it's quite true—anyone hearing the story would simply have said, "Batty old Lydia, mixing it again! Isn't it time she gave up?"'

With a wry smile Kate added, '"And why can't she let sleeping dogs lie?"'

'Yes, that seems to be the theme song.'

'I never knew they actually planned to *disinherit* Mark.'

'Neither did I.'

'We'd have grown up at Longwater, it'd be yours now.'

Daniel shrugged away such lost grandeur. Kate asked, 'Do you think Rosemary's telling us the truth or lying?'

'I think she's covering up. She wouldn't dream of betraying Grandmother's confidences, she's far too loyal. So she's . . . inventing a kind of censored version to keep us quiet. I think some of it's true, don't you?'

'Some, yes.' Her moment of revelation had lost its lustre. It was one thing to believe that Mark Ackland had cheated their father out of 'a considerable sum' of money, quite another to make him pay the money back. And if that had been Lydia's intention she must have had leverage at her disposal; she *must* have had the proof which her old friend had just told them she lacked. Kate now understood that if she couldn't find out what that proof was she'd be bound hand and foot, unable to move.

Daniel said, 'What are you thinking?'

She couldn't tell him; it touched too closely on the Blake Clinic and the cure which he dreaded. She said, 'The *ménage-à-trois* was a new one.'

'Oh God, I bet it wasn't only *trois*! What else did they have to do, all those idle layabouts and dodgy remittance men, whiling away their lives in hot countries with lots of cheap booze and bored women?'

'I can't see Auntie Helen joining in.'

'I can. She must have been a knockout twenty years ago, and apparently Mark was too.'

Kate glanced towards the house. 'The old girl's awake. Do you want to go back?'

'May as well. Who knows what she'll come up with next?'

But they had only taken a few paces between the pine trees before an obese figure came lumbering through the French window and advanced on them. One glance at his abundant curly hair told Kate that this was Sally's least favourite lawyer, Rosemary Howard's Andrew, and far from pleased to see them. Behind him the nurse was hovering about, red in the face. He said, 'I can't imagine what you think you're doing here, upsetting my mother.'

Daniel might have reacted calmly, but knew that his sister would do no such thing. 'Nonsense! We haven't upset her at all. She very sweetly asked us in for a chat.'

'The staff know perfectly well I'm to be kept informed of any visitors . . .'

'You weren't at home *or* in the office,' moaned the nurse, but he ignored her. 'I gather you're in possession of some letter she wrote. Please return it to me, it's her property.'

'It was found in my brother's house and it was written to our grandmother, I think that makes it *our* property.'

'Think what you like, I'm a lawyer, I'm talking about a point of law.'

'We'll have to consult our own solicitor, won't we?'

The round, once handsome face beneath the Byronic curls began to grow purple. 'Will you kindly give me that letter!'

Neither Kate nor Daniel missed the urgency behind the demand, it seemed to denote pure greed. They glanced at each other. Kate said, 'Absolutely not.'

'You'll regret this.'

'I doubt it,' said Daniel. 'The reference is Rex versus Kilmarnham, 1904.'

Andrew Howard's reaction, shock and incredulity, was a pleasure to behold. Spluttering slightly, he said, 'You'll oblige me by leaving here at once. And I don't advise you to come back.'

Kate stepped close to him and examined him with her iciest stare. 'Remember Sally Harding who used to look after my grandmother?'

'No, I do not.' But his eyes betrayed him.

'She nearly kicked you in the balls, and I wouldn't mind doing the same.' With which she pushed past him, calling out, 'Goodbye, Mrs Howard, thank you so much for seeing us,' and she and Daniel departed along a sandy path skirting the house. Out of earshot, Kate said, 'Rex versus Kilmarnham, did you make that up?'

'I don't think so. You know my mind—it collects all sorts of crap. Like those quotations.'

Parked in front of The Pines was a lordly dark maroon Mercedes, a convertible, obviously belonging to Master Howard. It's rear end, as wide as its owner's, blocked Kate's car so that she had to reverse on to the kerb and thump off it more than once in order to escape. Following this, her natural reaction was to swerve at speed into a glittering maroon side-panel, but she resisted such childishness.

Daniel said, 'Did you see that man's eyes? He was crazy to get his hands on the letter.'

'Yes, he was. I wonder why.'

They drove in silence, each occupied with their own thoughts which were for once widely dissimilar: Kate's fixed on Dr Allard's cure; Daniel's struggling with problems of analysis. After a long time, when they were on the motorway heading for Winchester, he aired his findings: 'It doesn't add up, does it? Something's missing.'

'Yes, the censored part of her story, if your theory's correct.'

'Maybe not correct but on the right lines. There must have been something bigger, nastier, than Mark diddling Father out of money.'

Yes, thought Kate, and within that 'something bigger' is the proof I need—intend to find. She kept quiet.

'The old girl wrote about a disastrous Pandora's Box and sleeping dogs being dangerous, both underlined. That couldn't have applied to Mark getting up to his old tricks which everybody knew about anyway.'

'So you said in the garden.'

'She's a devious old bird, she's no more vague than I am. Falling asleep was probably an act too.'

'She *is* eighty-three.'

'Then she threw in her *ménage-à-trois* as a red herring and fooled us both.'

'It could have existed, you said so yourself.'

'I'm not denying it, I'm saying she wanted to divert us from whatever it was she'd decided not to say.'

Although his line of reasoning was perfectly viable, Kate, whose priorities were practical, chose to find it irritating, no more than playing at detectives: irritating and in a sense negative, like his fear of going to California for treatment. She had to fight with herself not to argue with him; they both enjoyed, and occasionally indulged in, a good argument, but instinct told her that what might occur now would not fall into this category. It would be pointless and possibly vindictive; her temper might overcome her, and then wounding things would be said, initially by her, no doubt, but Daniel's tongue could be just as sharp: presumably they both took after Lydia. No, none of that. She kept quiet and so did he.

And thus they might have remained, at loggerheads, had not Daniel's bladder started playing up some ten miles short of Woodman's: a tiresome adjunct of his condition. They found a leafy spot and even a place just off the road to park the car, and he heaved himself away into the undergrowth while Kate paced to and fro, stretching her legs but not easing her mind. It happened when he'd returned and they were both back in the car, her hand on the ignition key. There was the sound of an approaching vehicle, and seconds later a dark maroon Mercedes convertible flashed by right in front of their noses. They both gasped. Without hesitation, Kate switched on, gunned the engine and, with a quick glance over her shoulder, shot out into the road, following.

Daniel said, 'Something tells me I'm not going to believe this.'

'I'd believe anything of that bastard.'

Had the driver of the Mercedes been in a hurry he might have lost them in a couple of minutes, but he was not in a hurry, and anyway it was a twisting side-road where nobody would have cared to drive fast in an expensive car. So, without the least difficulty, and obviously unrecognized themselves, they followed Andrew Howard at a discreet distance until he swung in at the majestic gates of Longwater House.

Brother and sister glanced at each other, differences forgotten, identical blue-grey eyes bright with excitement and surmise.

CHAPTER 5

The sight of Andrew Howard running to The Cousins in order to report on his mother's afternoon guests, with particular emphasis on the letter no doubt, had the most unexpected effect on Kate: it resolved all her uncertainties.

Pacing about the little living-room at Woodman's, while Daniel in his wheelchair mixed drinks, she demanded, largely of herself, 'And why not *ring* Longwater? Because he didn't want anybody overhearing what he had to say, that end or this.'

'Could be.'

'Which proves it's something potentially dangerous.'

Daniel nodded uncomfortably.

'And remember—Grandmother *did* consult him about her suspicions, whatever they were. He came right here to Woodman's, Sally saw him. So if those suspicions were important, more important than Rosemary was admitting . . . You suggested that yourself, Daniel.'

'I'm not denying it.'

'Did he go scuttling over to Longwater *then*? Good God, I'd have thought Lydia was a better judge of character.'

'You're right, she was.'

'Well if he did, you see what it means, don't you? The Cousins would have known exactly what Grandmother had up her sleeve. And if it was really threatening, something that mustn't on any account leak out . . .' She came to a stop, staring at the heavy newel-post which terminated the banisters: and it was indeed all jagged corners, as Sally had said. 'Daniel, if that was the case I can believe Mark came over here and killed her, I really can. Did you know this is what did it? Hitting her head on this ugly thing?'

'Sally again?'

'Yes.' She went over to the table and stared at him with fierce eyes. He pushed her drink towards her but she ignored the gesture. 'It makes sense of a lot of things which make no sense otherwise.' And, in a kind of fury: 'Oh Daniel, admit it, don't just sit there looking po-faced!'

'All right, it makes sense, but it's based on a hundred "ifs".'

'I'm sick of reason, something in my gut tells me it could be the answer.'

'It *could*, yes.'

'So the original happening, incident, whatever you want to call it, did take place when Mark and Helen were living abroad. Rosemary Howard was telling the truth about that. The roots of it are in Corsica.'

'Or Italy. And Kate, it was all a long time ago, maybe twenty years—they've been back in England for over ten.'

'What's twenty years? People remember—specially odd or unusual things.' And, with absolute finality: 'I'm going there, Daniel, I'm going to find out what went on.'

Her brother's head jerked up and he spilled some of his gin and tonic. 'Kate, you can't!'

'Why not?'

'In the first place, your job.'

'I haven't had a holiday for two years. Only last week Alex was telling me to take one before the summer rush.'

It was no good his bringing up language as an impediment because her only academic distinction (or was it an extraordinary natural knack?) lay in that direction; but all the same he felt a baleful certainty that she should on no account do what she proposed. He pulled her down into the chair beside him. 'Come on, have a drink, you're not thinking straight.'

'What's the point in thinking straight about something as crooked as this? I want to find out what happened and why. And I want some proof, Daniel.'

'Kate, darling Kate, please listen to me. If you're right and Andrew Howard's over there at Longwater this very moment telling tales, and if there *is* something that's got to be covered up—OK, maybe including Grandmother's death—don't you see what it means? You'd be putting yourself in great danger. The practical thing to do is keep quiet, don't rock the boat, above all stop asking questions.'

'*You're* the one who's hyped on asking questions.'

'Not if there's any truth in what you're saying now.'

'I'm going, Daniel. OK, we'll play it cool, no one need know, but I'm damn well going.'

'I don't like it.'

'Then come with me.'

'Don't be daft, what good would *I* be?'

Kate was so used to his disability that she sometimes failed to take it into consideration at all, particularly when she was excited. His question shamed her, and she studied the thin face in silence for a moment. 'Oh God! Will you be all right on your own?'

'Of course. I always am.'

'But if that fat lawyer's telling Mark what we're up to ... Supposing he ... turns nasty?'

'I'd shout for Tom, wouldn't I?'

Not for the first time the thought of Tom Duff struck Kate with overwhelming relief. His parents owned the Woolpack, a free house, and somehow an unlikely understanding had arisen between Daniel and their son. Tom was very large, a rugby player of local distinction, with fair hair and a child's eyes and a nature so generous, so open, that Daniel had apparently, and more than once, revealed his true thoughts to him over an occasional half pint of bitter. Even the obvious pity which Tom felt for Daniel's crippled condition—and could in no way hide—was forgiven, counterbalanced by the certain knowledge that if ever Daniel needed help Tom would answer the call as fast as his Land-Rover would carry him.

Reassured, Kate said, 'We'll keep in touch, I'll ring you every night. There are things you'll have to do here.'

At this, her brother went so far as to bang the table with his fist. 'For Christ's sake, Kate, you can't go alone, anything could happen!' And then, struck by a brilliant solution, 'Of course, Steve! Take Steve.'

The words stopped her dead in her tracks, robbed of all impetus. She heard Steve's voice saying, 'OK, I'll book a couple of weeks in Shangri-La.' Daniel saw it all reflected in her expression. 'Have you and Steve . . . called it off?'

She nodded, miserable because of the fact itself, and miserable that she hadn't so far found the courage to discuss it with the only (other?) person in the world she loved.

'You never told me.'

'It's not . . . Yes, it *is* important, but it's something I'm learning to live with.'

'You were crazy about him.'

'I think we were . . . are crazy about each other.'

'Then he'll go with you.'

'No. Because I won't ask him. Don't worry, I can manage on my own.'

'But Kate . . . where are you going to start? Who's going to give you information?'

'I'll start at Cortiano, their place in Corsica. Why did they keep it on? I think there's a reason. And what about the *ménage-à-trois*? Who was the third person? I'd like to talk to her, or him.'

'That was just tittle-tattle, she used it as a red herring.'

'So you say, but are you right? For God's sake, something pretty shocking must have happened if Mark had to kill Grandmother to stop her talking about it.'

'He probably didn't, that was just a wild guess.'

'OK, I'm working on wild guesses from now on.'

Her brother ran both hands through his hair, making it stand on end. 'But what do you think you're going to *achieve*?'

She had managed to keep it to herself all day, but it had to be said, and this was the obvious moment. She grasped his hand and held it tightly. 'If there was money owing to Father it'd be yours now, you're his heir. I'm going to force bloody Mark to give it back to you.'

'Force Mark!'

'By blackmail if need be. Or perhaps he'd rather get sent up for murder.'

Her brother groaned. Kate said, 'That money's going to cure you, Daniel. If it's the last thing I do I'm going to see you *cured*!'

CHAPTER 6

The village of Cortiano was tiny, a huddle of red-roofed cottages hugging what might, in winter or early spring, be a small river, the kind which dried to a rock-strewn gully as the year progressed. The house sat above it on top of a hill. Once a farm, the sturdy outbuildings had been converted and incorporated into the dwelling so that now it had trebled in size without having appeared to do so. Neat rows of vines dotted the south and west slopes of the hill, while to the north and east there were olive trees, their leaves fluttering in a light breeze. At one point the rock broke from the soil and fell in a small cliff (or perhaps this was the quarry which had supplied stone for the buildings) and at the foot of it, cunningly constructed to look natural, was a swimming-pool: nothing artificially blue or geometrical, merely a glitter of water in a hollow of rock. Kate would have liked to go down to it and swim there and then.

She had parked her rented Renault in the shade of some pines; it was very small but could cope with Corsican gradients if given time; on all sides of Cortiano rose higher hills, and beyond them mountain slopes. She now sat on a rock, drinking Orangina and examining The Cousins' continental domain from the roadside above it.

In her imagination she'd visualized the place as being shut up, comatose in their absence, but there were men working among the vines, and the upstairs windows of the house were wide open, with bedding hung out in the sun to air. Whether the owners, or rather the leaseholders, were there or not, Cortiano was a working farm, a going concern. When she'd finished her drink Kate would go down—she had decided how to introduce herself—but whether she would get an answer to any of her questions was in the hands of chance; however, she felt optimistic, had felt optimistic ever since arriving—the previous afternoon—in Bastia some twenty miles away to the north-east.

Not that her first glimpse of the island had been encouraging. Even the coast of France had been enshrouded in a mysterious pinkish haze which thickened over the sea, so that by the time they were flying over Cap Corse, the northern tip of Corsica, nothing was visible except a few bare peaks and, further south, the higher spine of the island and a suggestion of sprawling forest.

The man sitting next to her gestured gloomily: 'Sahara.' She remembered then that once, even in London some two thousand miles away from that vast and savage desert, her car had been lightly dusted with Saharan sand.

The plane descended through swirling veils, to which the local beaches were adding their tithe of grit, and came in to a surprisingly smooth landing at Poretta, the small airport outside Bastia. A strong, hot wind was blowing.

When it came to the matter of hotels, Kate decided to throw herself on the mercy of her taxi-driver who, like his vehicle, seemed middle-aged and reliable. To her horror, since they were on a busy road, he turned right around in his seat and examined her; then said, 'You're not a tourist, you're a visitor, correct?' It was a nice distinction. He continued, but with his eyes on the road again, much to Kate's relief. 'The porter at La Résidence pays me a little something for every foreigner I take there, but he is Genoese and also a Communist, and the place is too expensive. I will take you to a small hotel, quiet, respectable, clean: you will like it.' He added as an afterthought, 'It belongs to my second cousin by marriage.'

In this one speech, had she known it, Kate had experienced all or most of Corsica. By and large the Hotel Univers was indeed what he'd promised, quietness to the Southern mind being entirely a matter of degree; at least it faced a one-way street which might halve the traffic noise. In any case, Kate asked for a room high up at the back, and was greatly pleased with her view over variously russet roofs and, naturally, a leafless forest of television aerials.

Like many people who prefer hotel rooms with as much air and light as possible, which, in old cities, usually means the top two or three floors, she was always a little worried by the idea of fire: disabled elevators, staircases thick with blinding smoke. No such fear here. Due to the haphazard angles of the ancient streets the houses behind the hotel were not set squarely to its back, and her room occupied the point of the angle; only some eight feet from her window was a neighbouring roof: a flat terrace criss-crossed by clothes-lines from which a fat woman with grey hair was at the moment unpegging her day's wash. She smiled and waved a plump hand. Kate returned the greeting. In case of fire she could jump the gap with ease. Conversely, of course, anyone wishing to enter her room could do the reverse, but this didn't worry her; she had few valuables and always carried them in her shoulder-bag.

All in all she was mildly pleased with the way things had gone so far; she had always rather enjoyed travelling alone, and her French had come up to scratch with barely a mistake. Of course, an attractive girl on her own in any Mediterranean town must always run an intense gauntlet of male attention, but in the past she'd found that much of this was a kind of macho-formality, even in a sense good manners. How much worse it would have been to find oneself ignored.

Immediately opposite the hotel, which had no bar or

restaurant, was the Café l'Oasis. It was somewhat shabby and apparently patronized only by men, but there were two women behind the counter, and if suggestive comments were made upon Kate's entrance, these were quickly stilled by a savage look from Madame, a natural blonde of perhaps forty with unusual black eyes, a handsome face, and an air of authority; with perfect tact she coerced this rare female customer on to a stool near the till where she could keep an eye on her *vis-à-vis* 'the boys': for Kate now saw that this was very much a haunt of 'the boys' of various ages, some of them quite obviously the town's leading rogues.

Anna, the other woman behind the bar, was perhaps thirty, dark and pretty and a great favourite with the clientele; when she moved, Kate immediately noticed that she had a painful limp, and, getting the measure of the place and the men who frequented it, guessed that it was sympathy for her affliction as much as admiration for her prettiness which made her popular.

Needless to say, she reminded Kate of Daniel, and the thought of him re-aroused a sense of urgency. She intended to begin her investigation first thing in the morning, and so asked Madame if she knew where Cortiano was. No, she didn't, but in a raised voice which easily carried to the furthermost corner of the bar where there was a small billiards table, she consulted her customers for information. One—a hulking youth in his twenties—replied, 'Way up beyond Campile on the road to Grossa.' In reply to Madame's raised eyebrows, Kate said, 'I have relations there, I'm going to visit them.' The young man added that he'd be happy to give mademoiselle a lift in his van any time she wanted; this generated some laughter, as did Kate's reply, 'I'll take you up on that when I know you better.'

Madame, whose name was Françoise, directed her to a good inexpensive restaurant: 'Owned by another Pied

Noir—I am one myself. You know? Algeria?' Kate knew.

Altogether she enjoyed her evening, a pleasant change from the rich and pompous ambience of Hill Manor; as she returned to the hotel she noticed, with no surprise, that a fiery argument was now taking place in l'Oasis, shouted insults, a thumping of tables and much uninhibited laughter. She would like to have gone back there to take a look, but doubted if Madame Françoise would have approved.

Now, the Orangina finished and the examination of Cortiano completed, there was nothing to stop her embarking on her quest. She drove down a twisting road into the valley, passed through the village—closed shutters and flaking walls which no doubt concealed spotless interiors—then over a bridge and up another winding track which led to the farm and ended in a wide expanse of gravel facing the house. She took her time getting out of the car because she wanted to be observed by anyone caring to do so; she felt that this would probably be the best way of meeting whoever had been left in charge during The Cousins' absence.

She'd been expecting some kind of peasant farmer, but there appeared in the open doorway a dapper figure wearing black corduroy jeans tucked into black boots, a scarlet shirt and an expensive black leather jacket; the tanned face was intelligent, quick-eyed. 'Mademoiselle?'

'I just came to take a look at the place. I suppose I expected it to be closed, but when I saw . . .' She gestured to the men working in the vineyard, to the bedclothes airing at the windows. 'My name is Ackland, Kate Ackland.'

'Ah, a relative of the owners.'

'Cousin.' And, knowing the scope of this word in French parlance, she added, 'Monsieur Mark is my uncle. I understood they held a lease.'

'They do, but "owners" is less complicated, and they came here long ago.' He indicated the front door and she preceded him into a cool, shadowed hall: the original stone floor and beams, some pieces of what she took to be ancient local furniture, gleaming with polish and age. Extreme simplicity which surprised her. But why? Helen had taste.

'Mademoiselle would like to look around?'

'Yes, I would.' She hadn't really dared hope that he might say, 'Help yourself, I've better things to do,' and he did not. 'Looking around' meant a guided tour. He introduced himself as Jacques Lombardi. In spite of his quiet manner she had no doubt that he was a man to be reckoned with. Perhaps she'd been wrong to give him her real name, but it had seemed the most direct route to acceptance. She realized that he was assessing her as busily as she was assessing him, and perhaps more acutely; and he was adept at the evasion of leading questions. When she commented on the surprising number of bedrooms—from outside the house looked smaller—and added, 'A wonderful place to entertain—I'm sure they make the most of it,' he gave her a strange, dark look and replied, 'Some of the outbuildings are now staff quarters. My wife and I have a pleasant flat on the other side of the courtyard, facing east.'

The rest of Cortiano was as simple and as pleasing as the hall, with a beautiful sitting-room which could, by sliding huge modern windows, become part of a wide terrace, part of the whole valley beyond. A middle-aged woman was polishing furniture and brass fittings. It was here that Lombardi, perhaps rather pointedly, asked Kate when she'd last seen the Acklands. Kate could reply in all honesty, 'Last Monday. Uncle Mark and Aunt Helen, and two of my cousins, Giles and Miranda.' Very subtly, he had put her on the defensive: she *sounded* defensive, even to her own ears.

But at her words the woman turned, smiling; was on the point of speaking when Jacques Lombardi gave her a look so sharp that it might well have drawn blood. The defensive posture did not come naturally to Kate, and this tiny incident roused her to the attack; gently, and with a laugh, she said, 'Why, Monsieur Lombardi, you're quite evasive about them, aren't you? Have I stumbled upon some terrible family secret?'

His dark Corsican eyes flashed at the mockery, largely, Kate suspected, because the woman had not been able, or had not wished, to hide an equally mocking smile. It seemed reasonable to suppose that Lombardi would not be all that popular with the staff; doubtless he ruled them severely, perhaps harshly. 'Ah, mademoiselle, you tease me. But I have an important responsibility here. I take it seriously.'

'I can see you do. I know my uncle has absolute faith in you.' And, riding on this, she found she could quite easily turn to the woman and add, 'You were about to say something, madame.'

'Ah, mademoiselle, it was hearing the names of my little ones, Giles and Miranda.' And, noting Kate's surprise, 'I was their nurse, nurse to all of them. Gianetta, they still call me Netta.'

'Of course. I've heard of you. Miranda said I was to give you their love.'

'Bless her. And Giles, he has become a handsome young man, eh?'

'Oh yes, just like his father.'

Lombardi cut sharply across this feminine chit-chat. 'No doubt you would like to see the cellars where we make the wine.' He glanced at his watch. 'It is nearly one o'clock. My wife is a superb cook, and superb cooks demand punctuality.'

Kate nodded and said to the woman, 'Perhaps we'll talk again. Gianetta's an Italian name.'

'Oh yes, mademoiselle, I'm Italian. I came here with them from Italy.'

Kate turned away from Lombardi who would certainly have caught the excitement in her eyes, even if he couldn't interpret it. Wasn't this exactly the kind of lead she'd been hoping for? Netta, who had come with Mark and Helen Ackland from Italy. Perhaps the fact meant nothing; perhaps it was a vital link.

During her tour of the cellars—not her first experience of the mystique of viticulture—she was abstracted, wondering how and when she could resume her talk with the Italian woman; she knew her preoccupation didn't show; if running a hotel had taught her nothing else, it had taught her how to carry on a conversation while considering half a dozen other subjects.

She noticed that Lombardi managed to time the itinerary so that it ended at one, on the dot, when he approached a large bell bolted to the side of the house and tolled it six times, liberating his workers for their lunch-hour. He then escorted her to her car and did not say that he hoped to see her again; it was as if, by a strange osmosis, the air of duplicity which emanated from The Cousins at Longwater had been transferred to this foreign place, to this foreign man; or was it that they, being what they were, had employed Jacques Lombardi because they sensed in him a made-to-measure lackey?

He held the door for her, closed it upon her once she was in the driver's seat, and then stood there waiting to witness her departure. Kate was irritated; she'd hoped that he would hurry off to his superb luncheon, leaving her free to walk back into the house and find Gianetta who, she was sure, would have liked to ask more questions about her 'little ones'. Did she live in the staff quarters on the other side of the courtyard, or perhaps in the village? In any case, Kate now had no option but to drive away. Lombardi raised a hand in farewell. Kate ignored it.

But as things turned out she needn't have worried. If

Netta wanted to continue their talk she had her own means of ensuring that the talk continued; on rounding one of the corners of the track which twisted down through the vineyard, Kate came upon a placid figure sitting on a rock under an olive tree, knitting a sock. As she braked to a standstill she noticed that, at this point, the house above them was out of sight. Netta glanced up over her flashing needles, and Kate sat down beside her in the shade. With the heat of midday, even so early in the year, cicadas were sizzling and sawing all around them.

'I think,' said Netta, with true Italian chauvinism, 'our Monsieur Lombardi never forgets that Bonaparte came from this island.'

Kate laughed. 'He's not very welcoming. I don't think he liked me.'

'That was fear. He felt that you'd been sent by the family to spy on him.'

'I hope your talking to me like this won't get you in trouble.'

'Hah! Firstly he can't see us here. Secondly it would take more than Jacques Bigboots to come between me and Madame.'

'She likes you.'

'Didn't I bring up all her little ones? And also my husband runs the vineyard and runs it well. Until he came here the wine was vinegar. Now it is good, sometimes superb. Monsieur Mark is proud of his wine.'

'So you came from Italy with my uncle and aunt.'

'When little Giles was only three weeks old. Corsica, I thought, that is barbarian country. But Madame insisted, and now I like it here. I met my André, he has a temper but he's a good husband, we both work at the house, and Monsieur Bigboots gives *us* no trouble.'

Kate said, 'I'd forgotten Giles was born in Italy.'

'At La Spezia. I was lucky to get the job, I was eighteen,

I knew nothing. But my cousin was a maid at the villa there—ah, she was a liar, that Julia—and she said to Madame, "I know the perfect nurse, young but well-trained." Madame could see that I had no training at all, but I loved the little one and she liked me. So . . .'

Kate was thinking: La Spezia, wasn't that a big, ugly town: a port, factories, hardly the kind of place Mark and Helen would have chosen to live? She asked, cautiously, 'Where were they before that? I think they'd been living in Italy for some time.'

'I think so too, but I only met them then, at La Spezia. The girls were born here at Cortiano.' She glanced at Kate with a touch of canny surprise. 'Didn't you know that?'

'Yes. But I'm almost the same age as they are, remember—children don't think much about such things.'

'No, of course not. *Oh!*' A hand flew up to her mouth. 'You are their cousin, and your father was Monsieur Mark's brother who was killed in the auto crash.'

'Yes.'

'How stupid of me! And your brother is still . . .'

'Crippled, yes.'

'Ah, *il povero, il povero!*'

Kate realized that she was walking yet another tightrope. This woman owed a great deal to Mark and Helen Ackland, and her life was in many ways dependent on theirs, but all the same, she felt that there was a frail bond between the two of them, sitting here in the shade, serenaded by cicadas. It was very possible that too many questions, too pointed, might meet with resistance, even silence, yet those questions had to be asked, for this Italian woman knew the answers to many of them. She needed an excuse and had no time to think up a good one; she said, 'Netta, I'm not at Cortiano by chance.'

The other nodded, knitting-needles clicking.

'There has been . . . trouble in our family. Someone . . .

is making threats and demanding money, and we must know who it is. My aunt and uncle are too busy; I've been sent to see what I can find out.' It was the best she could do on the spur of the moment. She waited in some anguish for a response.

Eventually Netta said, 'No one here, no one at Cortiano.'

Kate breathed again; to some degree at least her story had been accepted. 'Why are you so sure?'

'I know them inside out. Lombardi is the only one who might try such tricks, but he wouldn't do it. With all his faults he's a decent man, loyal.'

'That's what I thought.' She let the implication sink in; and added: 'Yet this person obviously knew them when they were living abroad. If not here, then in Italy.'

Netta laid her knitting on her lap and turned her dark intelligent eyes on the girl beside her. Kate understood that it was this intense scrutiny, not the acceptance of her flimsy story, which would decide whether or not she was to get any answers. Feeling base, but also feeling that the end must justify the means, she met the regard with her own clear eyes.

Netta smiled. 'Your reason for asking questions is no concern of mine—we all have our own reasons for what we do. But I'm not a bad judge of character and I know you're honest. I also know that when he was a younger man, Monsieur Mark was foolish, wild, sometimes worse than that. He made many stupid mistakes and many enemies, and he was in trouble over money more than once. If he's being threatened now, it's no surprise to *me*.'

Kate was astonished at this burst of candour, and could not hide the fact. Netta grimaced. 'Now you think *I* am being disloyal, but I'm not. It is Madame for whom I have a great regard. I find Monsieur Mark . . . unfriendly, I'd be lying if I said I like him.' She picked up her knitting again. 'And I think you're right to ask questions in Italy. I think something happened there.'

Kate's heart seemed for a moment to have stopped beating. 'At La Spezia?'

'No, no—before I met them. Only later, when we'd come to Cortiano did I think this. I'll tell you why. It was . . . as if they were hiding from something or somebody. They asked no one to their beautiful house, no guests, not even from England. And they hardly went out at all themselves.'

'But . . . how long did this go on?'

'Years. Seven, eight years. A few local people perhaps, and a few children for Giles and Lucy—Miranda was a baby. I felt so sorry for Madame, she liked to entertain, she didn't enjoy always being alone.'

Kate was silent. This was an entirely new aspect of The Cousins in exile. She had always imagined a busy and sometimes raffish social life. She now realized that her questioning of Jacques Lombardi had been woefully inept; she had even mentioned all the entertaining they must have done at Cortiano. No wonder he had given her that odd, dark look, and had thereafter seemed suspicious: there had been no entertaining of any kind.

And what had Rosemary Howard said, sitting there on her high-backed chair in Bournemouth? 'Things didn't get any better abroad. More scandals, oh dear, yes! And he was taken to court by some Italian family . . . that curious *ménage-à-trois*.' So if there had been this solitary monastic existence at Cortiano—eight years, for God's sake!—they could well have been taking refuge from something which had occurred in Italy between their leaving England and their arrival at La Spezia. It was that trail which she must follow from clue to clue, like some childhood treasure hunt in reverse. It covered a span of several years, and she hoped the object of her search did not lie very far back in time;

she had two weeks' holiday—which might be extended to a third—and not a great deal of money.

Her relationship with Gianetta had at some point lost its early reticence, and she felt she could now say quite frankly, 'First I will go to La Spezia and see what I can find out there. Where did you all live?'

'In an old villa on the road to Portovenere, with a beautiful view across the bay. But last time I went to see my cousin it had been pulled down to make room for ugly apartments.'

Of course, the cousin, Julia, who had been a maid at the villa, and had inveigled young Gianetta into her job as nurse. She said, 'Perhaps your cousin would remember something.'

'Julia will remember everything. Oh, but she was a terror—listening at keyholes, and the questions she'd ask point-blank, I don't know where she got the nerve!' Obviously Julia was the card of the family, for Netta was laughing at the very thought of her. 'Yes, go and see Julia, I will give you her address. Perhaps I will even telephone, in the cheap time, to tell her you're coming.'

But as they parted she was serious again, eyeing the English girl with true Italian acumen. 'You should be careful in what you're doing. Italy is a man's country, it would be better if you were travelling with a man.'

'I'll manage. I take care.'

Netta nodded. It struck Kate that she had not believed one word of the story so swiftly invented as cover for so many peculiar questions; and it was remarkable (perhaps remarkably Mediterranean in character) that disbelief didn't inhibit her in any way. The story had been 'convenable', one of those French words which flummox the dictionaries, meaning so much more than 'correct' or 'proper': meaning, in this case, a passport to common feminine ground upon which they could meet and talk in comfort.

Upon this same ground, Netta could lean forward as they parted and kiss the smooth young cheek, saying, 'Take care. God bless you. I will pray for your brother. And in case you should worry—no word of what we've said will be repeated to *anyone*.'

Kate drove away deep in thought. She had no doubt that Netta would keep her mouth tightly shut, but she found herself wondering whether Jacques Lombardi—the good servant—would report her visit to his lord and master, Mark Ackland; it was an uncomfortable thought. Yet if she'd introduced herself under a false name, as a family friend perhaps, he would have turned her away forthwith; moreover she would never have found herself mentioning her cousins, Giles and Miranda, by name; and if she hadn't mentioned their names Netta would never have spoken, and their conversation under the olive tree would never have taken place. In fact, the visit would have been profitless instead of a mine of information. It seemed to her that she had gained a great deal by taking a small risk.

By the time she got back to Bastia it was three o'clock, and her stomach was telling her that she'd had nothing to eat since two croissants, with a cup of coffee, at breakfast-time. She went to l'Oasis and found that Madame was at home, dealing with her husband and sons, and that Anna was in charge. The place was empty except for two young men playing desultory billiards. Kate asked for a Croque Monsieur and a glass of Kronenbourg; when the girl brought them to her table she seemed inclined to linger. 'Did you find Cortiano, mademoiselle?'

'Yes. It wasn't too difficult.' She indicated the other chair, and Anna willingly sat down. 'You like our little bar, you like Madame Françoise?'

'Very much.'

'We see few visitors in here. It is perhaps too . . . rough for them. Françoise is a wonderful woman—God must have been watching over me that day, I had my accident just outside this door.'

Obviously she was dying to tell her story, and Kate had been curious about her from the start, realizing that she was not Corsican but Spanish. From Barcelona, it seemed. She had come to Bastia on a pilgrimage with a party of friends: by motor-coach to Marseille and then by ferry. They had wanted to pray at the church of Ste Croix where there was a miraculous crucifix which had been recovered from the sea under mysterious circumstances, a very holy relic. Anna had never left home before, and was so excited by the journey and by seeing the cross that she had paid no attention to Bastia's ruthless traffic; she'd been knocked down by a van which had crushed her right leg with both wheels: there, just outside in the street.

Françoise had run out of l'Oasis and, with some of her stalwart customers, had taken charge of the injured girl, going with her to the hospital, since few of her companions spoke any French at all. And then, for all the months Anna had spent up there, and throughout all the painful treatment, Françoise had come to see her *every day*. But when the happy moment came for her discharge, Anna had burst into tears, for how could she return to Barcelona and her humble job of office-cleaning? She couldn't even kneel down. And Françoise had said, 'You won't need to kneel down behind my bar, you can stand up and serve my customers.'

And so Anna had stayed in Bastia and become popular at l'Oasis and made many friends; and she owed it all to Madame Françoise—*that* was the kind of woman she was— and every week Anna went to Ste Croix to bless her benefactress and thank God for the way it had all turned out.

The simplicity of this story, and the teller's face alight with wonder, contrasted harshly with the circumstances of Kate's own pilgrimage to Bastia; and no sooner was she out in the street, wandering up the Boulevard Paoli, than her mind once again began to seethe with the revelations and surprises of her talk with Gianetta. They accompanied her on a stroll through the Old Town, where her eyes took notice of very little, and back to the Place St Nicholas. A ferry was just coming in to the New Port, and she realized that it would have been here, when first they came to Corsica, that Mark and Helen, the baby Giles and his young nurse, would have disembarked at the end of their short voyage from Italy.

Watching the ship, she thought for the first time that it was odd, since Mark was five years older than her father, and had been married five years earlier, that he and Helen had produced no child until Kate herself was already two. Giles, their eldest, had been born in the same year as Daniel. Well, on second thoughts there was perhaps nothing so unusual about it. Mark was a playboy and had been ordered out of England; presumably he and Helen were too rootless, too busy enjoying themselves, to think of settling down. Or perhaps Mark expected to be forgiven and recalled by his parents, and only when he and his wife realized this wasn't going to happen did they decide to find a home and have children: at Cortiano, as things turned out: Cortiano, their self-imposed prison. This was the most disconcerting thing she'd yet learned about their time abroad. 'It was as if,' Netta had said, 'they were hiding from something or somebody. They asked no one to their beautiful house, no guests, not even from England. And they hardly went out at all themselves.'

Had her grandmother stumbled upon the reason for this mysterious seclusion, thereby reanimating the fear which had led to it? And surely it must have been a very considerable fear to affect Mark Ackland so radically: that charming young reprobate who didn't give a damn for anyone. It would have been more like him to flaunt whatever monstrous escapade he'd got himself into, making a dinner-party joke of it. Unless, of course, he'd become involved in something criminal. But that couldn't have been the case, since he'd then made an obviously legal withdrawal to Corsica, a tenant of property at Cortiano and, as such, correctly registered with the Préfet's office.

Struggling with this convoluted problem, Kate went back to the Hotel Univers and up to her room. She took a cool shower, put on a minimum of make-up and a light dress, and was just picking up her shoulder-bag and a cardigan when it happened. There was a crash of breaking glass which made her wheel around in shock. Something was hurtling towards her through the unshuttered windows, net curtains flaring out into the room. At such moments time becomes meaningless, performing Einstein-ian tricks. Kate dodged, and the thing which was heavy struck her arm; glancing at the arm she found it covered in blood. Only then did she see what lay across her bed, eyes glaring into hers, teeth bared in a ferocious snarl: a large dog, with its throat so savagely cut that the head was almost severed from the body. Blood was spreading over the white counterpane. The dead animal had not quite come to rest; rolled over a little, with one red paw raised so that Kate thought with horror, 'My God, it's still alive!'

She didn't know if she had cried out. It was probable that she stood there, staring in disgust and terror for only a few seconds, yet they seemed timeless. Her room was suddenly stifling with the hideous smells of death, blood, incipient decay, excrement. She felt vomit rising in her as she turned to the door . . . and found she couldn't open it. For a moment panic, the idea of being locked in with *that*, blinded her to the obvious fact that she had locked it herself.

She turned the key and fell out into the corridor, mercifully deserted. She wasn't sure why she locked the door behind her: from force of habit or to distance the horror.

Only as she began to move away, fighting nausea, did shock seize her and throw her against one wall where she leaned, shuddering.

The roof-terrace of the house opposite had presented itself to her as an excellent means of escape in case of fire. Anybody, even she herself, could have heaved the dead animal from it and through her window: and probably without the friendly grey-haired woman knowing a thing about it. This was the only certainty her reeling mind could grasp; the rest was darkness streaked with blood. She fought another convulsion of vomit and managed to conquer it.

Again it seemed an age, but was probably a matter of seconds, before she was able to turn and stumble along the corridor towards the stairs; everything seemed to be swimming in and out of focus; the lift stood with open door, waiting for her, but she couldn't have borne to be imprisoned in that confined space; she ran unsteadily down the six flights to street-level.

The boy behind the desk was no doubt astonished to see her, frantic, blood-smeared, but before he could open his mouth she was pushing through the doors and into the street. She knew exactly where she had to go, it beckoned her with bright lights, l'Oasis. She ran towards it, looking neither to left nor right, and came within a few feet of suffering little Anna's fate. She burst into the café on a squealing of tyres and a flood of explicit Corsican vituperation.

Shocked faces confronted her, some of them no doubt recalling that other terrible accident. Madame Françoise took one look at the English girl's expression, the bloody arm, ran out from behind the bar and thrust her past dangling strips of plastic, straight into the tiny office which lay beyond them, at the same time calling out, 'Anna, cognac!'

She gestured Kate into the only chair, facing an untidy desk, shut the door and leaned on it. 'For God's sake, what happened?'

An oblique thought flashed through Kate's mind that such instant reaction to crisis came naturally to this woman. Algeria must have taught her to act so swiftly and to keep her head in an emergency. She herself seemed unable to find the correct French words, but they evidently sufficed. Staring at her with wide eyes, her handsome face grim, Françoise took the cognac from Anna, shut the door, and pushed the glass into Kate's hand. She said, 'Dear Jesus Christ, the Dog! What have you been doing?'

Bemused, Kate replied, 'Nothing. I mean . . . really nothing.'

Françoise shook her head decisively. 'On this island the Dog is not sent for nothing.'

CHAPTER 7

Although Daniel spent much of his time alone and was content to do so, Kate's sudden departure for Corsica left him feeling unusually restless, not so much lonely as undefended. No need to look for reasons, Kate had even mentioned one: they were embarking on a defiant course of action against rich and powerful people who lived less than a mile away over the hill. If his sister was even half correct in her hypothesis—if, for instance, Mark Ackland *had* been forced to shut his mother's mouth for fear of what she might say, he was going to be enraged and possibly frightened to find that so many years later a new generation was in pursuit of the same secret.

Like many crippled people, Daniel was seldom afraid; the accident and its endless aftermath had given him a blessedly fatalistic attitude towards life; but from a physical, practical point of view it was obvious that under certain conditions he'd be quite helpless, alone at Woodman's in the middle of nowhere. To be sure, he could always depend on his friend Tom; but supposing Tom wasn't at the Woolpack when the crucial moment arose—he could be miles away playing rugger.

Just at this moment, with his research for Dr Forrester completed and already posted off to Oxford, he had too much time on his hands for introspection. Whether or not he believed his sister to be on the right track, the least—and best—he could do would be to apply his mind to the same problem; and oddly enough, on the morning of her departure, something occurred which led him to a disturbing discovery.

It was not one of Ava's days for cleaning; he had made his bed, not too difficult since it only consisted of a duvet, and was about to go downstairs again, had in fact already sat on the miraculous chair-lift, when his eye was caught by something he'd never consciously noticed before even though he must have looked at it a thousand times. The sturdy post at the top of the stair-rail had at some point been capped with a plain wooden knob which didn't match either post or banisters. He looked at it for a few seconds, and then at the foot of the stairs where the corresponding post was surmounted by that heavily carved newel upon which, according to Kate, their grandmother had hit her head in falling.

He had not visited Lydia at Woodman's more than half a dozen times during the years she'd lived there, and when he concentrated on the matter he could remember the plain knob: something solid and comfortable for an old hand to grip before beginning the descent; but—and now he was quite sure of it—he could also remember, perhaps from his very first visit, that there had once been a matching and equally hideous newel crowning this top post as well. And it wasn't all he remembered. When he'd first moved to the cottage, he and Kate had stored in the attic some of his excess possessions and several unnecessary pieces of furniture which merely got in the way of his wheelchair; and unless he was very much mistaken . . .

It was by no means an easy operation for him to carry out alone, but at least the trap door to the roof space was opened by pulling on a rope cleated to the wall of the upstairs landing, and, by the same mechanism, two sections of aluminium ladder then slid forward and downwards. This contraption may have been put in for his grandmother's convenience, in the days when she could still see a little, but was even more of a necessity for Daniel; without it, the attic would have been inaccessible.

Climbing the ladder was in any case something of an undertaking, but dependence on his arms had made them very strong, and his comparatively 'good' leg helped considerably: though once again he realized, with a pang, how much weaker it was getting. He reached for the light switch and revealed the usual attic clutter: not only his own boxes and the unwanted furniture, but several rotting deckchairs, croquet mallets, hoops, balls (croquet at Woodman's! There wasn't a flat piece of ground for miles), abandoned picture-frames, an old ironing-board, cartons of unwanted kitchen implements—he had brought his own—and piles of magazines and pieces of wood, supreme fire hazards, including chair- and table-legs, golf-clubs, a torn garden sunshade, and . . .

He hauled himself forward to look more closely. No, his memory had not played him false; there lay the top newel, an ugly and heavy piece of carved wood identical to the one at the bottom of the stairs. Moreover, it had once slotted into a hole in the post, now covered by the knob; had indeed slotted deeply into it, some nine inches. When Daniel picked it up, this thick wooden pin fitted into his hand with ease, so that the whole thing suddenly became a weighty club.

The idea popped into his mind as effortlessly as it would have occurred to his sister, famous for jumping to conclusions. If somebody had hit Lydia Ackland over the head with this weapon, the wound would automatically have presented itself to the Coroner's doctor as having been caused by the old lady's head striking the bottom newel-post. *If!* Only two days ago, when Kate had said she could easily believe that Mark might have killed his mother, Daniel had replied that her theory was 'based on a hundred ifs'. And here was another which his pragmatical mind could both accept and refute. He did not as yet have enough evidence, not even circumstantial evidence, to make any accurate judgements; and neither did Kate herself who ought, at this moment, to be crossing the Alps at thirty thousand feet. Time would instruct both of them.

Time, in Daniel's case, took him first of all into the local town where he visited his bank. Since shopping was always easier in the village, where he and his disability were well known, he stopped there on his way home, and afterwards went to the Woolpack for half a pint of bitter. He was too honest with himself to pretend he'd gone there for any other reason than that uneasy sense of being undefended which had haunted him all morning: or, since they were so closely intertwined, the equally disturbing thought that Kate was putting herself in a far more undefended position.

Either way, Tom's large presence behind the bar was reassuring. Daniel always felt that his friend's world was so extrovert, so blithely uncomplicated, that nothing untoward could ever occur within it. He said nothing about how he was feeling, having promised Kate to keep quiet about her journey and thus her absence, but something was understood between the two young men. Tom felt, without analysis, of course, that Daniel would not have come in for his bitter without being motivated by some obscure reason (to Tom, Daniel was in every way an obscure person) and he took it for granted that Daniel must sometimes feel lonely. As a matter of fact, he couldn't imagine Daniel ever *not* feeling lonely, stuck up there in the woods on his tod, but it seemed he seldom did.

So, as usual, it was an encouraging encounter for both of them, the simpler character liking to feel needed, for whatever reason; the more complicated one comforted by the fact that if he should want help it was not all that far away.

This interdependence was forcibly emphasized when Daniel returned to Woodman's and at once realized that the place had been searched: unprofessionally searched. There was hardly a paper in his desk, a book left lying on the arm of a chair or a newspaper on the table which didn't reveal to him the clumsy hand of an interloper. Because he was an ordinary—if private—young man, his immediate reaction was one of rage; because he was painfully crippled, an ever-present guardian grabbed the rage and subdued it, advising caution: stealthy caution perhaps, but caution none the less.

He had no doubt at all that this was the fourth step in a sequence, starting with Kate's ill-advised visit to The Cousins—continuing with their joint, and perhaps equally ill-advised, journey to talk to old Rosemary Howard—which had led directly to her son's arrival at Longwater. If Kate was at Woodman's right now, Daniel realized that he'd be arguing with her because she would have jumped to the conclusion that Mark himself was the intruder; but he was in the habit of arguing with her in order to steady her flights of fancy, he was the self-appointed tail to her uncontrollable kite. Alone, he could drop this role and admit that there had been no breaking and entering, not even a token pretence of it, therefore a key had been used, therefore Uncle Mark, or someone dispatched by him, had searched the cottage.

For what? Andrew Howard knew that they were asking questions about their grandmother's death, and he knew that they'd shown Rosemary Howard the letter she'd written to Lydia—the letter he'd so desperately wanted to possess. The fact that this letter was the sole piece of actual evidence surely proved beyond a shadow of doubt that it was the object of the search. Daniel congratulated himself on his own foresight; Rosemary's letter had been his reason for visiting the bank that morning; it now reposed in his deposit-box.

He ate some bread and cheese and drank some apple juice, not reading as he usually did, but staring out of the window at what had become a cloudy day, and wondering what the next move might be. A visit, he decided, from Uncle Mark Ackland. He found himself wishing that Kate was going to be there to lend moral support; on the other hand, if moral support turned into loss of temper, it was perhaps just as well that she was now, if her flight was on schedule, just setting foot in Corsica.

Following these thoughts he wasn't in the least surprised to hear the approach of a distant vehicle which he presently identified as Mark Ackland's Range-Rover. Since the accident and his imprisonment in a wheelchair Daniel was used to people looming over him, but when his uncle's massive shoulders filled the front doorway he did wish, for a second, that he'd been standing up with his crutches. Not that they made him any less vulnerable, rather more so, but being, in theory, on his own two feet tended to give him confidence. From the look on Mark's face, brown from weather, red from lunch-time wine, confidence would have been an asset.

'Hello, Daniel. How's Kate?'

'Fine. Back at work.'

'No point in beating about the bush. When she came to

see us the other morning she mentioned you'd found a letter here—to my mother from an old friend . . .'

At least there'd been no phoney-polite conversation: straight to the point—with a whopping great lie. It was on the tip of Daniel's tongue to reply, 'Kate never mentioned it, Uncle Mark; Andrew Howard did.' The response would be fascinating, but he held his tongue; the physically weak know how best to preserve their mental advantages.

'As you'll appreciate, it's my property. Like everything else that belonged to Mother.'

Daniel allowed himself to think about this for a long time, watching his uncle's growing irritation; then he took a leaf out of fat Andrew's book by saying, 'I should've thought it was the property of the person who wrote it.'

Because Mark Ackland had become accustomed to the role, among others, of bluff land-owning gentleman, it didn't mean that he was quite that simplistic under the surface, and he now realized that the bluff approach was not cutting any ice with this intelligent cripple. He smiled, charmingly, as he knew, pulled up a chair and sat down. Assessing the smile, Daniel thought it was easy to see, even now, what an attractive young man he must have been: yet quite unlike their own equally attractive father, so often the way with brothers. 'Not,' he was saying, 'that there's anything important about the letter, as far as one can tell. I just thought I'd like to have a look at it.'

Considering how boring and frustrating it must have been for this man to search the cottage without result, Daniel thought his uncle was putting a pretty good face on it. He said, 'To tell you the truth, I'm not sure where it is. I *think* Kate gave it back to Mrs Howard.'

It was a clever move (he was a good chess-player) because Mark Ackland had purposely not mentioned their visit to Bournemouth in order to conceal his source of information; and here was his nephew taking it for granted that he knew all about it anyway. Daniel could almost see him wondering whether this meant that he'd somehow traced Andrew Howard as the source of information, and if so, how? He also saw Mark take the middle ground, choosing to say, 'I'm not sure it's any of your business, either of you.'

'Well,' replied Daniel judicially, and, as he knew, maddeningly, 'as you say, it wasn't an important letter. We were just interested—after all, she *was* our grandmother.' He knew that this utterance could be interpreted in several different ways, from the ingenuous to the obliquely threatening. And he could now witness further anger overcoming his Uncle Mark who was doubtless thinking that this bloody little cripple and his sister had actually seen the letter, whereas all he had to go on was a second hand account of it from a dodgy lawyer, who also hadn't seen it and was basing his own information on the word of an ancient mother; and she (as Daniel himself well knew) was capable of anything from downright misinformation to loss of memory. Not a strong position on the board.

In as smooth a voice as he could muster, Mark Ackland said, 'If your sister gave it back to Mrs Howard you'd remember, no doubt about that. So I don't think she did anything of the sort. Which means, my dear nephew, that you're lying to me.'

Daniel spread his hands. 'I can't stop you thinking whatever you like.'

'Frankly, I find your attitude bloody insolent. Has it ever entered your head, you can only afford to live here because I charge you virtually nothing?'

'Yes, I'm very grateful.'

'I could chuck you out tomorrow.'

'Not tomorrow,' replied Daniel. 'We have a contract. April the first next year.'

His uncle leaned closer; Daniel could even smell the stale aroma of the lunch-time wine. 'I want that letter.'

'I'm sorry, I wish I could give it to you—particularly with eviction staring me in the face.' His heart was pounding, but he was damned if he was going to be bullied by this arrogant old brute.

In a much quieter voice, Mark Ackland said, 'You're a damn fool. There are worse things than eviction, you'd better consider *that*!' He pushed back his chair and stood up; then turned to the door which slammed behind him.

Daniel grimaced to himself. Certainly there were worse things than eviction: like being hit over the head with a great chunk of wood and thrown downstairs. He had no idea how far his uncle would go: quite a long way, he now suspected. Too many years of being top dog, lord of the manor with friends in the very highest of places, had warped his sense of values—which must have already been misshapen by a dissolute youth. 'Justice, *c'est moi*,' seemed to be the attitude, and a very dangerous one it was; he, Daniel, would have to be a great deal more cautious than he'd supposed.

Not that he *felt* in the least cautious; in fact, he was surprised to find that his whole attitude had changed. The searching of his cottage, and now the threatening interview just ended, seemed to have obliterated all those logical arguments with which he'd felt compelled to counter Kate's wild guesses and even wilder reasoning. He found that he too could now believe that Mark Ackland might have killed his own mother, and could sympathize with his sister's determination to go to Corsica. He wasn't quite sure why they'd embarked on this unequivocal course of action. Kate's idea of raising money to send him to the Blake Clinic still struck him as fanciful, but he could recognize a tyrant when he saw one, and was glad they were defying the old monster; he had no intention of running away from the consequences.

However, when he considered his situation more carefully, he came to the conclusion that he *was*, in this case, a little afraid. And the answer to that was to take steps; he wheeled himself to the table, put on his glasses, and wrote three short notes stating that if anything untoward or suspicious should happen to him, or conceivably to his sister, urgent inquiry should be instigated, starting with Mark Ackland of Longwater House; and it might be no bad thing to inquire at the same time into the death of Mark Ackland's mother, Lydia. He addressed these to his ex-army stepfather, Alistair, in Aberdeen, to Alex at Hill Manor Hotel, and to his bank manager: all honourable men who would obey the instruction not to open them unless something highly suspect occurred.

Then he heaved himself out to his little car, drove down to the village and posted them. After this he felt a lot better; but there was no doubt in his mind that before very long his uncle would bring some sort of pressure to bear on him. All he could do was sit and wait; experience had made him good at sitting and waiting.

CHAPTER 8

Kate found herself telling Françoise the whole story of her visit to Corsica and the events leading up to it. Having cast herself on the Frenchwoman's mercy in so melodramatic a manner she could hardly do less, and in any case, she trusted Françoise. During her recital the bloody mask of the dog, purple tongue lolling between yellowed teeth, kept sliding into her mind, and it seemed she'd never be rid of that stench of animal death.

Françoise, black eyes bright, nodded once or twice at what she heard, but it didn't seem to amaze her unduly. Perhaps its operatic overtones did not seem all that outlandish to the Southern mind: hatred between two brothers, disowning of one of them, tragic death of the other, mysterious secret possessed by the old grandmother who might or might not have been killed for it . . . In Mediterranean lands the passions ran high and were seen to run high: none of that furtive reticence which was responsible for some of the more stalwart, as well as the more unpleasant, aspects of the Northern character.

In the meantime, Françoise had dispatched Mario, one of her reprehensible but loyal customers, to the Hotel Univers armed with Kate's key; he was to pack all her belongings, pay her bill, answer no questions, give no information, and return to l'Oasis as quickly as possible.

Kate noticed that even he seemed to have paled slightly following his encounter with what lay on her bed, but perhaps this was only because he, like Françoise, knew the meaning of the Dog. She said, 'You obviously realize that it indicates death. I've never heard of an incident where death hasn't followed the Dog. Sometimes soon, sometimes late, but always.' She drank a little cognac. 'However, you don't live here, and for you I think it means something slightly different. It's a warning, and I'm quite sure that this man, Lombardi, is behind it, acting on instructions from your charming uncle in England. It says, "Leave Corsica, and stop inquiring into matters which are not your concern." You agree?'

'Yes. But I'm not going to stop.'

Françoise regarded her very seriously; then there blossomed on to her face that singular smile which so altered her entire personality. 'I too would refuse to stop. For the same reasons, I'm sure.'

'They wouldn't try to scare me off unless I was on the right track.'

'Exactly.'

'It was a hideous experience, and I'm sorry I've put you to all this trouble, but . . . Yes, I'm glad it happened.'

'Don't be too glad, it's not over yet.' She leaned forward to emphasize her point. 'You plan to go to La Spezia?'

'Yes.'

'Between now and the moment you get on that boat you must on no account be seen by *anyone*.'

'But . . .'

'No buts. I will take you to my sister's house. She has a flat she lets to tourists in the summer.' She held up a magisterial hand to forestall argument. 'And please—no more English nonsense about giving me trouble. It is one of your countrymen's least appealing characteristics, this refusal of help before it's even given.'

'You seem to know us very well.'

'My second lover was an Englishman—your Consular Service. A charming man, but we weren't compatible except in bed. Which brings me directly to the other thing I must ask, and I beg you to listen to me. It was brave of you to embark on this investigation alone—I would have done the same. But you have put yourself in great danger. The Dog may follow you.'

She could see that the image thus conjured up struck Kate with horror: padding feet, the slit throat, the terrible stench, following, following. She took swift advantage of it, adding, 'You must send for a man. You're an attractive girl, there are men you can trust.' Netta had said the same, and Françoise received the same answer: 'I'd rather not.'

'Then you're more of a fool than I am, and I wash my hands of you.' She leaned back, brandy glass under her nose. 'Men are not *very* useful,' she conceded, 'but sometimes they're essential. They think practically. We *can*, but we tend not to.'

Kate nodded. Françoise would be surprised at how few men she actually knew, but in any case there was only one she'd consider asking for help—Steve. And she was irritated with herself to find that even in this near-disastrous situation the idea of seeing him again overwhelmed her with excitement.

'If,' added Françoise, reading her expression with accuracy, 'he is a lover, so much the better—he will protect you more effectively. Telephone him.'

'Now?' panic gripping her.

'Certainly now.'

'He's a very busy man, he may not even be in London.'

'Ring him, my friend.'

If Kate had decided on the spur of the moment to call Steve from Hill Manor or Woodman's he would have been out, or in New York, or at a conference in Edinburgh, and his answering-machine would have instructed her to leave a message after the bleep. From Corsica, where communication with mainland France was by no means infallible, at an awkward hour of the evening, with Françoise eyeing her ironically, he of course answered on the second ring—he must have been sitting at his desk or lying on his bed.

'Steve?'

'Kate, for God's sake! I was thinking of you at that very second. Where are you?'

'Corsica.'

'Alone, I hope.'

'Well . . . yes—I mean, that's the point, Steve. I seem to have got myself in rather a mess, and I was wondering . . . It'll be terribly inconvenient, but . . .'

Françoise leaned over and took the telephone out of her hand. 'Monsieur Steve, my name is Françoise and I am her good friend . . .'

Kate had suspected, on being told about the Consular lover, that Françoise probably spoke some English: perfect English as it now appeared. How typically French that she'd given no indication of the fact. She was saying, 'She's not in rather a mess, she's in extreme danger and her life has been threatened. She badly needs your help, can you come to her? Good. Then you must fly Air France to Bastia airport, Poretta. Take a cab from there to a bar called l'Oasis, 56 rue Adamo. Have you got that? Ask for me—Françoise. Now I give her back to you.'

'Jesus!' said Steve's voice. 'Quite a woman!'

'She's that all right. But Steve, if you can't make it . . .'

'Of course I'll make it. What the hell have you been up to?'

'It's a long story.'

'Tell me tomorrow. I love you.'

Kate replied, 'Oh!' in genuine surprise. Laughing, he rang off.

Françoise said, in French, needless to say, 'Forgive my interruption. Calls to England are not cheap, and the British are often incapable of coming to the point. Particularly if the emotions are involved.'

Kate laughed. 'I owe you for the call anyway.'

'Not now. I will keep an *addition* of what you owe me, and we'll settle at the end.'

What followed was as incisive. Behind l'Oasis ran a narrow street, no more than an alley but large enough to accommodate Françoise's little Peugeot. Anna conducted Kate across a yard behind the bar and, on hearing the car, opened the gate. Kate got into the back seat and, feeling foolish, lay down, half on the seat, half on the floor. Françoise threw a travelling-rug over her, then a couple of empty wine cartons. Her suitcase was popped into the hatchback by the same Mario who had retrieved it from the hotel, and that was that.

Twenty minutes later they drove into the integral garage of a neat little modern villa at Alzetto, a mile or two north of Bastia and on a hillside overlooking the sparkling lights of the coast. Madame Jeanne Barbet, the sister, turned out to be as unlike Françoise—physically—as it was possible to be: a plump and amiable French housewife with curly brown hair and a fussy taste in clothes; but she was just as efficient, just as unfazed by circumstances. The flat was bright, adequately and sensibly equipped for vacationing parents with young children. It was self-contained, but an iron grille now covered the front door, and the only access was through Madame Barbet's own house. 'In any case,' said Françoise, departing, 'who knows you're here? Nobody.'

Kate had promised to telephone Daniel at seven; she was an hour and a half late, and knew how much he'd be looking forward to the call and how disappointed, even anxious, he'd be when it didn't come. So as soon as she was alone in the flat she dialled the Woodman's number. It rang three times and then stopped; a moment later she was nearly deafened by a high-pitched howl. It was the first time, *ever*, that she'd called him and not heard his voice almost immediately. Unsettling.

She tried the number again, and this time it didn't ring at all, neither did it howl at her; there was merely an eerie hissing silence. She told herself that it was quite possible that the phone was out of order, but something in her stomach derided the easy way out. She began to be sure that all was not well at Woodman's. She should never have left him alone there; she was mad.

On the day after his Uncle Mark's two visits, one clandestine, the other overt (which was also his sister's Day of the Dog), Daniel sat waiting for further developments. He was in a divided state of mind: the cautious Daniel, very much aware of his physical vulnerability, toyed with the idea of phoning his rugby-playing friend, Tom, and asking him to come up to the cottage as soon as possible; he would then explain something of the situation confronting him—not in all its complexity, which would only blow a fuse in Tom's mind—and act upon whatever advice Tom offered. If Mark Ackland returned, as Daniel was sure he would, it would be interesting to see him reacting to Tom's muscular youth and his size: the taller by at least two inches. On the other hand, a more devious Daniel was curious to know what his Uncle Mark's next move might be in pursuit of the letter, and even more curious to know how he himself might outwit this move. There was good sense in the first choice, and a shadow of hubris over the second. Hubris was naturally the more interesting option, it always is, hence mankind's record of stupidity.

Allowing arrogance and acumen to continue their age-old battle at the back of his mind, Daniel turned his mind to something which had been exercising him ever since his last conversation with his sister: Andrew Howard. Kate's theory was sensible and straightforward: their grandmother had, stupidly, consulted him over the secret which she was proposing to divulge, incriminating Mark Ackland. The lawyer had at once betrayed her confidence by nipping over to Longwater and relaying the whole thing to Mark. The result had been the death of Lydia.

What had been Andrew Howard's motive? There was only one which made any sense at all: he proposed to blackmail Mark Ackland.

This was where Kate's theory began to fall to pieces; it would not make sense for a blackmailer to go running *back* to his victim merely because Daniel and his sister had been to see Rosemary Howard with the now-famous letter. Andrew had certainly wanted to get his hands on it and, had he done so, might have used it at Longwater for his own base purposes; but he *hadn't* got hold of it, and still he'd gone dashing over to Longwater in his Mercedes, where he could have done no more than report on its existence; hence the search of Woodman's and his uncle's second, bullying visit.

All this suggested a theory somewhat different from Kate's. She herself had said, regarding their grandmother's consultation with Andrew, 'Good God, I'd have thought old Lydia was a better judge of character,' and he, Daniel, had replied, 'You're right, she was.'

That was the key. Lydia had sensed that the lawyer, son of her best friend or not, wasn't to be trusted and she hadn't told him what was in her mind. After this profitless meeting, Andrew had reported to Longwater, by pre-arrangement or with an eye on possible future gain. He had very little to say, and what he did say could have made no sense to him at all, he didn't possess enough pieces of the puzzle; but Mark possessed them all right and, fitting them together, knew that there was only one thing to be done: stop Lydia's potentially menacing mouth.

Daniel saw the puzzle analogy—a jigsaw-puzzle analogy—as fitting the circumstances to a T: not only the past and Lydia's death, but the present in which Kate in Corsica and himself in England were in the process of searching for a lot of important pieces which had fallen on to the floor and been lost; his new surmise regarding Andrew was only one such, of minor importance he had to admit, but it could lead to a revelation of the whole. It was this: the lawyer possessed no more pieces of the jigsaw than they did—rather less since he hadn't seen the letter and they had. He was therefore engaged in the same investigation as they were; was, in fact, an unwitting confederate who might possess interesting clues as yet unknown to Daniel and Kate. Daniel now saw it as his prime purpose to get hold of that information by hook or by crook. It was even possible that Andrew Howard, without knowing it, held the linking pieces which would reveal the whole design of the puzzle.

Meanwhile, the pleasant spring day of cloud and sunshine and drifting cloud-shadows continued towards noon, and passed it, with nothing happening to disturb the peace of Woodman's. Daniel relaxed somewhat and gave up the idea of summoning Tom's help: no longer activated by hubris, as far as he knew, but by afternoon torpor. He hadn't slept well the night before; waking or sleeping, his Uncle Mark's face tended to appear and reappear, and twice he awoke in fear having dreamed that he'd heard or seen the Range-Rover approaching stealthily through the woods.

The result of this was that after tea he felt his head drooping over the book he was trying to read; he took off his glasses, rearranged himself in the wheelchair and prepared for a nap. Both front and back doors were locked and only a very small window by the fireplace was open for fresh air. He felt secure. He slept.

It must have been the thump of the exploding petrol-tank which jolted him awake. The room was in half-darkness, due to a clouded dusk, but it was alive with the shuddering light of flames. He jerked his chair to the window and saw that his Mini was ablaze, sending up leaping swirls of fire out of all proportion to its size. The trees under which it was parked tossed their seared branches as if in agony.

Daniel's instinct was to go out and see what he could do in the way of rescue, but his second thought was naturally that in his crippled condition he could do nothing. He drew back from the window and sat hunched in his chair, biting the forefinger of his left hand, trying to marshal his thoughts. He had no doubt that his Uncle Mark was responsible, whether in person or by proxy didn't matter. A normal reaction might have been to call the police immediately, but the thought had only to flash across

Daniel's mind for him to abandon it. Mr Ackland of Longwater behaving like some common hooligan, the very idea! He could see the expressions of incredulity on the faces of the local constabulary.

In the past there had been undesirable elements hanging around the woods: once a stealthy infiltration of so-called travellers, encamped in filth: once an invasion of motorcyclists, all half stoned, zooming up and down the rides attired in black leather, like denizens of the pit: always poachers of different kinds. Uncle Mark would have a variety of scapegoats to hand: quite apart from the fact that Mr Ackland of Longwater House, friend of the lord lieutenant and twice as rich, was scarcely likely to play such tricks: and on his own nephew, a poor cripple!

Yet Daniel was sure that it had been Mark's doing; and, as surely, he was now isolated at Woodman's, a mile and a half from the village. The obvious intention was to scare him, and it had worked. He pushed his chair over to the telephone and dialled the number of the Woolpack. Tom would have him out of the cottage within fifteen minutes. It took him a short while to realize that the phone was dead: the line had been cut.

He had never doubted that his Uncle Mark really did mean to get the letter, but somehow the savage implementation of this wish was none the less shocking. A dozen or more visions of what might happen next crossed his mind, each more disturbing than the last. He doubted that Mark would actually take his life, but he couldn't excise from his memory the angry voice saying, 'You're a fool. There are worse things than eviction, you'd better consider *that*.'

The idea struck him almost immediately but he rejected it as out of the question, absurd. Obviously he must hide. Could the trap door to the attic be locked from the inside? No. And piling furniture on top of it, always supposing he could perform such a feat, would achieve nothing because it opened downwards in order to allow the descent of the ladder. There was nowhere else, no cellar, not even a sturdy shed. If he hurried, while daylight lasted, he could perhaps hobble a short distance into the woods, but then what? He couldn't climb a tree, and covering himself with fallen leaves would be worse than useless since the lord of the manor was always accompanied by one or more dogs which would immediately discover him. A year ago, perhaps even less, he could probably have got as far as the village on his crutches, but that was before the new deterioration of his serviceable leg. Now he knew he couldn't rely on it to give him the necessary balance. He would fall, and might not be able to stand up again.

At last, the rejected idea came sidling back into his mind in all its absurdity. Could he, somehow, in spite of various dips and one quite steep hill, and in spite of the way being far from smooth, make the journey in his wheelchair? No, no—out of the question! So what was the alternative? To sit here, waiting for Mark Ackland to arrive and continue the interrogation? His every nerve rebelled against that course.

Supposing there were men waiting outside, waiting for him to emerge? Well, supposing there were—what difference did that make: to be caught outside, at least making an effort to escape, or to be caught in here doing nothing?

Suddenly he was full of determination. Anything was better than supine inaction. He struggled into his coat, clamped his crutches to the side of the chair, picked up the flashlight which always stood on the table, put on his toughest gloves, then wheeled himself to the door.

If the Range-Rover were to approach it would use the south-western track which came directly up the hill from Longwater. The way to the village was at the back of the cottage, to the north; and, though rough, it clung to the opposite slope and was steep: dangerously steep perhaps, but think how quickly its gradient would remove him from Woodman's. He could do it, he *would* do it.

Perhaps the most alarming but by no means the hardest part lay in opening the front door. It was impossible not to imagine two large men, a couple of compliant gamekeepers perhaps, standing on each side of it. But there was no one. Daniel paused, listening. Only the normal night noises of the woods and a metallic creak or groan from his now burnt-out car. Heat from it wafted towards him with the smell of melted plastic.

Obviously the plan had been to cut off his escape and scare him witless; then allow him to stew in his own fear for a while; then pay a call and see if his attitude towards answering questions had perhaps changed. He pushed off from the door, circling without mishap the more or less level ground which surrounded the cottage, aiming for a break in the trees where the downhill track began.

Yes, it was steep all right, with a tendency to slope transversely, but he knew the chair well and could feel, almost as if it was part of his body, its reactions to tilt and balance; so far he wasn't even taking a risk, but still he leaned his weight in the opposite direction like a lone sailor in a strong wind.

It was by now getting dark, so that he had to sense as much as see what lay directly in front of him; the last thing he wanted to do was use his flashlight which, through the fine foliage of spring, would probably be visible from some considerable distance. The chair was a good one, solid, with strong brakes which he had to clutch very hard indeed against this steep hill. Daniel knew that at the bottom of it he would wish that he'd agreed to have an electrically-assisted chair, but they were awkward and heavy and he didn't like them.

Once, on a damp patch, he went into a terrifying skid and feared that he was going to turn sideways; the locked wheels would then topple the chair and throw him heaven knew how far down the hill, probably off the path. If he could recover at all from such a disaster, it would take him an hour to crawl back, perhaps right the chair, perhaps clamber into it again. Luckily the skidding wheels struck a stone, or the end of a fallen bough; the chair slewed around the other way, and Daniel just, but only just, prevented it leaving the track altogether, plunging downhill through undergrowth and finally, no doubt, wrecking itself and him against a tree.

At the bottom of the hill he stopped and listened again. A gust of wind stirred the branches above him and moved on. A fox was barking in the far distance. No other sound.

In the gully where he now sat, a good half-mile away from Woodman's, there was sometimes a stream, in winter a torrent. He wheeled himself carefully across its slushy bed, praying that he wouldn't get bogged down, and by exerting all his strength managed to climb out of it: a tiny rise which might as well have been a cliff. It gave him a foretaste of what was to come.

He knew his arms were very strong, but they had never been put to a test like this. The upward slope covered perhaps a hundred and fifty yards, and every inch of it was physical anguish. He pushed on the wheels and pushed again, and then jammed on the brakes and recovered. Then, again, a push and another push, and another grab for the brake. By God, if anyone came after him, and his tracks would be easy to follow, he'd be caught on this hillside like a fly on a windowpane. But no one came, there was no stomach-churning flash of lights, pinning him to the steep path; and so, push and ... push, and stop. Push—and push—and the brake.

The pain of the ascent ran through his arms like some brutal form of sciatica: his back began to ache, he could almost feel his spine buckling—and of course the torment wracked his pelvis and spread to his pathetic legs: insofar as they were able to feel anything at all.

He refused to look upwards towards the top, which was only a dark tree-mazed line against a paler sky, but concentrated on each push and push and rest, each push and push and rest. In spite of the gloves, his hands were already raw with blisters; he knew he was mad ever to have embarked on this exploit; he was snuffling to himself, half weeping with the pain, and then . . .

Then suddenly there was no more hill. He raised his head and found himself at the top of it. He wiped his nose and his eyes and looked up through the lacy branches to find that a new moon had sailed out from behind cloud; and for once he hadn't seen it through glass, so he wished with a vengeance, and began to put his wish into instant practice by pushing off down the long gentle slope ahead.

There were a few uphill stretches, yes, but they were nothing compared to that agonizing climb. He refused to allow himself to believe that he might after all do it, but the thought kept flitting through his mind, urging him on. His hands had started to bleed, making the gloves slippery.

Another hundred yards and, he estimated (for it was now quite dark, with only a glimmer of moonlight indicating the track) that he would come to the drive. Of course it would be a blessed salvation to turn on to the smooth surface and go that way to the village. The distance might be slightly greater, but how simple it would be, and all downhill. But instinctively he sensed it to be a dangerous route. Supposing a car were to come sweeping up or down the drive? Supposing his disappearance had been noted and the lodge-keeper told to keep an eye open for him? No, he would stay with the track; the going might be more difficult, but at least there would be no cars.

In fact, he was much closer to the drive than he'd

thought, and its exact whereabouts was revealed to him by the very thing which was urging him to avoid it; he saw, only some twenty yards ahead, a dancing radiance which, at the same moment as he heard the engine, became the full glare of headlights. There was nothing he could do. The hillside rose sharply on one side and fell away as sharply on the other. No friendly bush, no cover of any sort. If the driver, whoever it might be, so much as glanced to his right as he crossed the line of the track he would see the figure frozen to the wheelchair—could not fail to do so.

Hypnotized like a rabbit by the glare, Daniel sat unblinking, unbreathing. He could now see the actual headlamps flickering through the trees, the dark shape of the vehicle. It was on top of him, and there was no chance whatever that he wouldn't be seen. He waited in agony for the sound of hastily applied brakes . . . but it didn't come: only the sound of the car receding, slowing as it approached the lodge and the road beyond.

Daniel took an enormous gulp of cool night air. Glancing down the hill he could see, through trees, that the car had even turned away from the village. He gripped the wheels and urged the chair forward; it bumped across the hard surface of the drive and, slithering slightly, found the track on the far side of it. Another two hundred yards, and he could glimpse, below and ahead, the warmly-lit and welcoming windows of the first cottages. By God, he'd done it!

Minutes later he was in the back yard of the Woolpack, clutching his bleeding hands together, gasping for breath and looking up, far far up, into the face of his towering friend, Tom Duff. Tom assimilated the emergency at a glance and did something he would never have dreamed of doing under ordinary circumstances; he picked Daniel out of the chair and carried him into the back parlour; and Daniel, who would normally have been infuriated by such abject dependence, found that under these far from normal conditions he didn't mind at all.

When Kate had recovered from the shock of not hearing her brother's voice over the telephone, and when, at her fourth attempt, a maddening recorded voice told her that the line was out of order, she immediately thought of the Woolpack; found her address book in the disordered depths of her shoulder-bag, looked up the number, and so at length spoke to Daniel, some half an hour after his arrival at the pub.

She listened, with growing anger, to his story; after which he listened, with irritating lack of surprise, to hers: it was exactly the kind of thing he'd expected all along. Moreover the time factor made it clear that his last two visits from Mark Ackland were divided by Lombardi's report from Cortiano concerning Kate's sudden appearance there. The destruction of his little car, no less than the shocking arrival of the slaughtered dog, were the results.

Kate was expecting him to plead with her to come home and forget the whole thing; the fact that he did nothing of the sort, coupled with an uncharacteristic air of truculence, made her realize that recent events had radically changed his way of thinking. She said, 'What I can't understand is why he's come out into the open like this—trying to scare us both off.'

'Pure bloody arrogance. He despises us, he always has. Half-witted cripple and his sister who works as a chambermaid in some hotel.'

'*He* must be the one who's half-witted.'

'Arrogance usually is. He feels a hundred per cent secure, Kate. Did I go to the police when he destroyed my wretched little car? Of course not, he'd have had a cosy chat with the chief constable, wouldn't he?'

'But he's given himself away. He's told us there *is* a secret and he's not going to let us get hold of it.'

'That's right. Arrogance again. If it came to our word against his he knows who'd win.'

With only a trace of hesitation, Kate said, 'I . . . I've asked Steve to come here. You were right, I can't manage on my own.'

'Good.' He had never been one for I-told-you-so. 'Then what?'

'Italy. What we're looking for happened there, no doubt about it. What are *you* going to do?'

'The Duffs want me to stay here, keep my head down, until my hands are OK. I can just about use the crutches, but I can't touch the chair.'

'It's too near Longwater. You know how they talk in that village.'

'The Duffs don't talk.'

'Doctors do.'

'I'm not having a doctor, Tom's dealing with it. All that mayhem on the rugger-field, he knows what he's doing.'

'Bless him, give him my love. But Daniel, we've got to be careful. You've just told me how powerful Mark is—don't go underestimating him.'

' "Be bloody, bold and resolute; laugh to scorn the power of men . . ." '

She was glad he was still able to quote, even in his present predicament, but she had to reply, 'I know that one. *Macbeth*—and look what happened to *him!*'

Next morning Daniel called Ava, his cleaning lady, and said he wouldn't be needing her for the rest of the week because he was going away, they'd settle up later. Meanwhile Tom drove up to Woodman's in search of clothes, books, and a few other odds and ends which Daniel needed. If Mark Ackland or any of his henchmen appeared, he intended to ask for Daniel, register surprise at his absence and depart.

As things turned out, he came back with the required belongings and the news that the lock on the front door had been changed, thus rendering Daniel's key useless. Asked how he'd got in, he smiled his innocent smile and said, 'I leaned on the back door a bit. Worst pair of bolts I ever came across—just fell off.'

Later that afternoon, lying half asleep on his bed, Daniel found that Andrew Howard had slipped back into his thoughts. It had been his intention to suggest a peaceable meeting; he still felt that fat Andrew might unwittingly hold information which could be added to what he already knew. But now it occurred to him that he hadn't given nearly enough thought to the matter. Apart from the unlikelihood of the lawyer agreeing to see him, peaceably or not, anything he might know could only have been gleaned from his mother. It was evident that Rosemary Howard had no intention of betraying any of Lydia's secrets, but the fact remained: she was the one who knew all there was to know, and moreover she was far more likely than her wily son to reveal an important clue.

Daniel saw his course quite clearly now; he must get Andrew safely out of the way for a few hours and then make a return visit to The Pines. He began to consider ways and means.

CHAPTER 9

Steve lay flat on his back in the large *matrimoniale* of their safe house, Jeanne Barbet's flat for holiday-makers. He was fast asleep. Kate, propped up on pillows, watching him, wasn't surprised that he was exhausted; merely grasping the chain of events which had taken place since the discovery of the letter would have been enough to exhaust anybody, quite apart from the rest of an unusually busy day. In sleep he looked boyish, life's lines of tension and determination smoothed away.

Naturally everything had changed between them. She had called for him, and he had come eight hundred miles to help her. Their meeting, their embrace under the sympathetic but watchful eyes of Françoise and her sister, had been oddly formal and, left alone together, they had not, as in the past, hurled themselves on to the bed, locked together. Something in both of them said, 'There's time. Things are different now.'

Kate had realized, even as she was telling him her story, and most of Daniel's too, that the journey to Corsica, the bizarre results of it, her asking for his help and his so readily giving it, had in some way eased her away from the old life; it seemed inconceivable that she would ever return to Hill Manor, and inconceivable that she had not realized straightaway that somehow or other her future lay with this man.

Their lovemaking, when finally they came to it, provided further proof: so gentle, so natural, so sure of itself, and so satisfying. 'See?' it appeared to be saying, 'you're made for one another. I told you at your first meeting, and you've been fighting against me ever since. Don't worry, human beings have always been fools.'

She pulled the pillows down to the horizontal and let her body lie against his. He muttered, turned on his side and put an arm over her. Her last thought before she too slept was, 'Tomorrow we'll be in Italy.'

Steve, having fallen asleep first, woke up first, still entangled in a dream which was more than half a memory. There had been a time, at school, when teenage fashion suddenly dictated black. Everybody appeared in black. But he had no money to spend on clothes and had continued to wear his old jeans, suffering the usual merciless mockery because of it. Then the idea had come to him; he possessed a pair of white jeans, and a white shirt, and an old pair of white shoes which he cleaned up; and so, next day, turned up all in white. His contemporaries were too astounded for mockery, and he, looking like some ad for washing-powder, had turned on them laughing, calling them a lot of mouldy old crows, asking them where the funeral was. It didn't change the fashion—only fashion does that—but it shut their mouths, and he learned a lesson which had served him well ever since: if you can't join 'em, beat 'em.

He turned to look at Kate beside him, silky hair tousled on the pillow, dark lashes flickering a little on the smooth cheeks. One breast lay outside the bedclothes; he kissed it gently, not wanting to wake her.

What a story! Dead dogs being thrown through windows, and that crippled brother trapped, alone in a forest miles from anywhere, and all because some powerful, obviously deranged berk had ordered intimidation by dog-slaughter and car-burning. Perhaps you should expect such Gothic antics once you started defying the moneyed classes, let alone the semi-aristocratic ones. Well, Steve knew a great deal about *that* little lot; had spent half his business life learning how not to be rude to them, whatever the provocation, while at the same time hoodwinking them in every possible way.

For their part, they'd seldom missed an opportunity to let him know that they considered him a common and pushy upstart, if quite bright. As a result he had no respect for them whatever. Come to think of it, if Kate needed help against the Upper-Middles, with all their constipated shibboleths, she could scarcely have summoned a more knowledgeable or relentless ally. It would be a positive pleasure to trip this overbearing bully-boy, Mark Ackland, and rub his nose in it.

He was still a little surprised by his own unquestioning

acceptance of Kate's appeal. He could easily have said, 'But I'm leaving for New York tomorrow,' it would have been the truth. He was amazed he hadn't said it, and in that moment he'd realized, as Kate had realized upon their reunion in this room, that it was useless to pretend they could exist apart from each other. If Steve Callender, of all people, could for one moment risk his career for another person, then that other person had to be momentously important.

Not that in the end he was taking too much of a risk anyway, provided he could be back in London within five days, six maximum. Maddon, one of his juniors, had been about to depart for Turin; to his delight he'd found the trip switched to New York. Steve had explained to the managing director that there might be trouble with Guido Amari, who was getting too big for his boots: he wasn't sure Maddon could deal with Signor Amari, and proposed to go himself. So, somehow or other, if Kate's adventures allowed, or even if they didn't, he must spend at least a day in Turin.

Looking at her now, so childishly vulnerable in sleep, he was amazed all over again that she'd embarked on this dangerous quest merely because she hoped it would lead to money which might be used to cure her brother's disability. Very few men or women in the world he inhabited were capable of such loyalty and unselfishness. Added to these virtues was, he'd been surprised to find, a tough acerbity which would drive her to defy her Uncle Mark to the very end, no matter what form that took. Quite a girl! It seemed to Steve that they might go far together.

Both Françoise and Anna came down to the ferry to see them off: an odd pair, one so tall, blonde, untidily elegant, with those sombre dark eyes, the other so small, with black Spanish hair standing out in a frizz around her pretty face. Anna had brought a bottle of good French cognac as a gift from herself and some of 'the boys' from the l'Oasis, those with a spare franc or two in their pockets. They must not on any account, she said, drink Italian brandy which would rot their stomachs.

'Perhaps,' said Françoise with the rare and surprising smile which so transformed her austere good looks, 'you will come and spend a holiday near Bastia. Perhaps even your honeymoon. I will find you the perfect little place to stay.'

Kate shied away from the word 'honeymoon', but Steve, at his engaging best, replied, 'Why not?'

'And take care of her,' added Françoise, 'or some of my customers will not be pleased.'

Steve, who had seen the customers in question on his arrival the night before, assured her that he wouldn't like to displease any of them.

And so they sailed for Italy.

After a good deal of thought Daniel telephoned Booth, Howard and Lord, Solicitors, of Bournemouth and asked if he might speak to Andrew Howard. He was kept waiting, but then Andrew was the kind of man who would keep everybody waiting as a matter of principle; he wasn't yet successful or rich enough to eschew this small man's gambit, and probably never would be.

'Howard here.'

'This is Daniel Ackland. We met outside your mother's house, you may remember.'

'I most certainly do.'

'I've been thinking about that meeting, Mr Howard.'

'I'm glad to hear it.'

'We consulted our solicitor, and you were perfectly wrong in claiming the letter belonged to your mother because she wrote it. That would have been the case before it was posted and delivered, after which it became our grandmother's property—but I'm sure you know that.'

'Well...' Faint but unmistakeable sound of a lawyer climbing down. 'I was ... upset, you know how it is.'

'The point is that it struck my sister and myself that we really have no *use* for the letter, it's not even of any sentimental value...'

Faint sound now of breath being inhaled and held.

'... and as you seemed so keen to get hold of it, we thought we might hand it over to you.'

'That would be generous of you, Mr Ackland.'

Daniel had hitherto doubted Kate's contention that this man intended to use the letter to blackmail Uncle Mark; he almost wished he was really going to let Andrew Howard have the thing; on the other hand, he and Kate might yet use it to deliver a much harder and dirtier blow. He said, 'I'm staying with friends in London at the moment. I believe you come up from time to time.'

'Frequently.'

'So I thought perhaps we could meet and I could hand the letter over to you. I don't like the idea of sending it through the post.'

'No, no. A meeting would be far better.'

'What day would suit you?'

'The sooner the ... I see from my diary I've rather a busy week, but I'm free tomorrow. Why don't you have lunch with me?'

'I'm sorry, I can't manage lunch. How about a drink beforehand?' He was thinking of Rosemary Howard's rest from two until four p.m.; he would have to visit her in the morning.'

'Perfect. Let's make it ... twelve o'clock at the Savoy.'

'That'll be fine.'

They bade each other a cordial farewell.

Midday in the Strand. Even if Andrew Howard travelled

by train his journey would take over two hours, and at a rough guess he could be relied upon to arrive half an hour before their meeting. Add half an hour, at least, of irritated waiting when Daniel didn't appear; say an hour wasted in London, probably much more, followed by another two-hour journey home. That gave a minimum of five and a half hours; more if the pompous clown decided to drive in his expensive car; in any case, Daniel wanted no more than an hour's conversation with Mrs Howard.

He would now check train times, and as soon as Andrew was out of the way tomorrow morning he'd ring The Pines for an appointment. He had no idea what he expected to discover; but he was sure there were treasures buried there and, with luck, he might turn up a diamond or two.

Kate and Steve arrived in Italy at lunch-time after what seemed an interminable crossing. They rented a car from Hertz, a small blue Fiat, and drove straight to the Hotel Bobbio in La Spezia, as recommended by Françoise. During their voyage they had discussed in detail the time and money at their disposal, coming to the conclusion that they could afford to waste neither. Therefore Kate immediately rang Cousin Julia at the telephone number given to her by Netta; she didn't expect to find her at home and, even if she was, didn't want to interrupt the sacred siesta. '*Siesta!*' cried Julia on a burst of laughter. 'Oh my God, you will see!'

What they saw, after finding the place with some difficulty—it lay at the edge of the town—was children. Julia had five of her own in evidence, which, since she must have been about forty, meant other older ones elsewhere; she was also minding another four belonging to a neighbour. Bedlam, rather than siesta, was the order of the day.

Netta's cousin was an attractive woman, fleshy, even voluptuous, with dyed red hair and a laughing face. Since she wore nothing but a flowered cotton shift, a great deal of the flesh was on show, including, from time to time and depending how fiercely one or another of the young ones was mauling her, a pair of fine breasts. But there was nothing coquettish in this; she took her ample body for granted, and since she found it the most natural thing in the world, which after all it was, the occasional disclosure of it became natural too.

Her little box of a house, cheek by jowl with a couple of dozen others, would in a Northern climate have been deeply depressing, but few things are depressing in brilliant sunshine under an Italian sky; they had moved here, she explained, because her husband worked at the cement factory, an ugly collection of concrete slabs which dominated the area.

Obviously she had an eye for an attractive man, insisting that Steve, with his black hair and eyes and dark complexion, must be Italian. His inability to speak more than a few words of her language amused her greatly, and, winking at Kate, she proceeded to call him by several ripe and suggestive nicknames. It was impossible not to like Julia.

Opening a bottle of Valpolicella and brushing aside children, she explained that Netta had indeed telephoned her last night, as she'd told Kate she might. 'So you're interested in Signor and Signora Acklan', eh?'

Kate replied, 'Yes. It's a . . . rather complicated family matter: they're my uncle and aunt.'

Julia smiled over her wine. 'Netta told me not to ask awkward questions, so I won't.'

'It was a long time ago you worked for them,' suggested Steve, haltingly. 'Perhaps you remember little.'

'Oh no, Signor Handsome, I remember everything.' She sighed. 'It was the last work of that kind I did. I enjoyed it, I enjoyed having a finger in other people's pies. More interesting than having babies and cooking.'

Kate said, 'There were just the two of them?'

'And the little boy when he was born.' The dark eyes had suddenly become sharp. 'Why? How many did you expect?'

'Well . . .' Kate shrugged. 'At one time I believe they were travelling with a third person.'

'Yes, they were.'

'For some time perhaps.'

Julia nodded. 'I too got that impression. Many months.'

'I don't know if it was a man or a woman.'

'It was a man . . .'

Kate and Steve exchanged a glance.

' . . . but he never came here, to La Spezia.'

'Then how do you know . . . ?'

Julia gave her great laugh. 'Signorina, if you don't ask me how I know, I won't ask you why you ask such questions. In those days I was a mad bad girl. I kept my ears open, and my eyes. Enough?'

'Enough. Then this man stayed at . . . at the place where they'd lived before they came here.'

'He had no choice, he died there.' And, while Kate was still staring in surprise, 'I saw them set off for the funeral.'

'Julia, where was this place?'

'I don't know, they never spoke of it. Strange, uh? They spoke of everything else when I was around, but never of that place, and only once of that man.'

'Do you think it was near here?'

'Yes, I do. Because they went to the funeral in a big black car with a chauffeur. They had money, I know, but to have gone far in a thing like that would have cost the earth. One would take the train or fly, and have the big car meet one. Yes?'

'Yes, of course.'

Steve tried again. 'You said they speak once of the man?'

'Ah, you're coming along, but not "speak", "spoke".'

And then, frowning: 'I couldn't understand them. You know how it is—if you don't understand what's going on, the subject, words have no meaning. She said something like, "Mark, he *wanted* to die. I'd have felt the same, wouldn't you?"—something like that.' She paused and looked into her wine, drank it and added, 'I think the man who died was her lover.' And when Kate glanced up sharply: 'Now that's a guess. I know nothing, I heard nothing, but women . . . You know it yourself, there are certain things one senses.'

She picked up a small girl, disentangled her clinging arms and put her on the floor with a light spank on the bare bottom to indicate 'Off!' Then said, 'Also, you see, the funeral was only a few days after they'd come to San Matteo—that was the name of the villa, and I hadn't got used to their ways.'

'A few days! I'm surprised you were there yourself—I mean, they'd hardly had time to employ you.'

'I was there when they arrived, the owner kept me on when she left. They weren't the first of her tenants I'd looked after—but they were the most strange, that's why I remember them so clearly.'

In English, Steve said to Kate, 'They must have left this first place very soon after the other guy's death.' Kate translated. Julia shrugged. 'I don't know. If the . . . the dead one *was* her lover, the husband could have taken her away, men do things like that. Also . . . I shouldn't say this—I can see Netta's face, she thinks I'm shocking—but I thought then that perhaps this other man, not Signor Mark, was the father of the little boy. Ah, will God forgive me for saying such things? I confess it often enough, my confessor doesn't seem to mind.'

'Probably enjoys it,' said Steve, grinning.

'All right, I will say this too—Signor and Signora

Acklan' came here to *escape* from the other place. They were . . . awkward, how do you say it?'

'Ill at ease.'

'Yes. All the time they were at San Matteo. And then, only three weeks after the boy was born what do they do?'

'Corsica.'

'Again escaping.'

'So how long did they stay at La Spezia in all?'

'Six weeks, no more.'

Kate was shaking her head in bewilderment.

'Just enough time to pick up my Netta and they were gone.'

'But Julia, why?'

'I told you, they were afraid. And that's another guess, I'm a wicked woman. You ask me, I say what I think—God gave us brains, didn't he? Listen, I will tell you. My husband's brother is a stupid fellow, always in trouble with the carabinieri. Once he stayed here in this house, hiding, for three days. It was the same feeling at the Villa San Matteo—hiding, escaping, fear.' She raised both hands and let them fall again.

Kate said, 'This place where they lived before they came to La Spezia, we have to find it.' She knew that the urgency in her voice was not lost on the other woman, and had no doubt that her husband would be entertained to a fine, mysterious story when he came back from work.

'There are a thousand small towns, villages in the hills of Liguria, a hundred within a few miles of La Spezia . . .'

It was the name 'Liguria' that touched something in Kate's memory, but at the moment she couldn't grasp it. She said, 'Julia, there must be some small clue, something they said.'

Julia frowned and thought for a while. 'Yes, they . . . they spoke of a contessa. More than once.'

'Spoke of her in what way?'

'Now you remind me, I . . . I thought that perhaps the house they'd lived in, before coming here, was owned by this contessa, just as Villa San Matteo was owned by a doctor and his wife. A letter came one day when I was cleaning windows, and Signora Acklan' says to him, "It's from the contessa. Apparently we owe her for the telephone," something like that, I forget. Telephone or perhaps electricity.'

Liguria, Kate was thinking, Liguria?

It came to her in the car when, having thanked Julia and said goodbye to swarming children, they were trying to find their way back into town. She and Daniel had been talking to Rosemary Howard in Bournemouth, and the old lady had spoken of Liguria: 'Gerald and I loved Italy, particularly Liguria.' And then her sudden remark about the *ménage-à-trois* had diverted them both, and while they were pursuing an explanation which wasn't forthcoming she had specified some village. Her voice sounded again in Kate's memory: 'Are you sure it was Corsica? I thought Italy, I'm sure Lydia mentioned . . .' Yes, there had been a village, perhaps two villages, and Kate could recall neither of them. But according to Rosemary, their grandmother had actually named them in connection with what she had discovered about Mark: about Mark having cheated their father out of 'a lot of money, a very considerable sum'.

Somehow or other all the threads seemed to be drawn together at this unknown point not too far from where they now were: Mark and Helen Ackland—old Lydia's suspicions which may have been fatal—Rosemary Howard's muddled, or possibly mock-muddled memories—a contessa who was owed for a telephone bill—a maid who saw and heard too much—a man who had died and whose funeral Mark and Helen had attended—their retreat to this town and their further retreat to Cortiano—all, all drawn together at a village with a name Kate could not remember.

Daniel was the one with the memory, and Daniel also made notes. She prayed that he'd done so after they'd left The Pines, seen off the premises by a rude and angry Andrew Howard. She would ring him as soon as possible.

Steve, who had been lost in thought, or perhaps merely lost in the maze of one-way streets which blocked any approach to their hotel, said, 'What were they scared of? Why were they hiding? You don't suppose they'd killed the other man?'

'I don't know. If he really *was* Helen's lover . . .'

'Is Mark the jealous type? He sounds it.'

'But they'd been travelling around with this man for a long time—they must have been great friends.'

'*Something* funny happened at the contessa's house. If Julia's right and that's where they'd been living.'

Kate nodded. 'It's there, Steve, I'm sure of it—all there.'

'Ah, but all *where*?'

'I've an idea Daniel can tell us, if we ever get to a phone. Haven't we been down this street before?'

'We've been down this street, dear Kate, three times, this is the fourth.'

When they finally reached the calm of their room at the Hotel Bobbio, Kate immediately telephoned Daniel at the Woolpack. Tom Duff answered and called him at once; he laughed when he heard his sister's inquiry. 'Funny you should ask—I'm going back to see Rosemary tomorrow.'

'What about filthy Andrew?'

'I've arranged for him to be elsewhere. And of *course* I made a note of what the old girl said, I make a note of everything. Hang on a sec.' The sound of rustling pages. 'Sleeping dogs lie . . . all the past had been forgotten long ago . . . Ah! She said, "I'm sure Lydia mentioned Lasetto or Lazzetta, something like that."'

Kate wrote down the two names, at the same time asking, 'Are you all right? No more trouble with Uncle Mark?'

'Doesn't know where to find me, does he? Let's hope he doesn't know where to find you, either.'

'He can't, not that quickly.' She wished him luck in Bournemouth, he wished her luck in Lasetto or Lazzetta.

Steve spent ten minutes at the porter's desk and came back with the answer on a slip of paper. 'No Lasetto around here. Lazzetta is about twenty-five miles away up in the hills, near a place called San Pietro Vara.'

She hugged him excitedly. 'It's only four o'clock, we can go there now.'

'Bit late for dropping in on people.'

'But we can find out if it's the right place—if they were really there. Perhaps we can even discover where they stayed.' And, sensing slight reluctance: 'Steve, this could be the answer to the whole thing, we must *know*.'

Steve, who had been thinking more in terms of a comfortable half-hour with his feet up on the bed, next to hers naturally, could only capitulate, laughing at the excitement. He hoped that when they got to this place she wouldn't find rows of shaking heads and hands outspread in incomprehension.

Lazzetta may have been only twenty-five miles away, but reaching it was no easy matter. In the first place they found themselves funnelled on to the *autostrada* when their intention had been to pass under it; so there they were, trapped amid tons of hurtling metal and going in the wrong direction. Moreover, there was no escape for some thirty miles, at Sestri Levante. But in the end this didn't turn out to be quite the disaster it seemed, for the little town of San Pietro Vara, their point of reference, was actually nearer to Sestri than to La Spezia.

It was one of those still evenings, golden yet glittering, which the Mediterranean only produces in spring, and as they ascended out of the dark pine woods they came to a barer, more ancient-seeming landscape, scattered with terraces of olive and vine and narrow strips of agriculture. But when Lazzetta came in sight, sprawling down a hillside in the late afternoon sunlight, it was a complete surprise to them: not the crumbling peasant village they'd been expecting, but a small town, very neat and orderly, with its own police station and an absurd *fin-de-siècle* town hall, fallen into disrepair. The wide main street was lined with plane trees, already in full leaf, and the *piazza* at the end of it sported a wondrously involved fountain: mermaids and tritons and a buxom lady, Venus perhaps, rising from their midst; this dated from the period of the town hall and was unfortunately just as abandoned; it was also waterless.

In fact, the fountain was symbolic, for this had once been known as Lazzetta Terme, one of those diminutive spas so dear to the Italian heart. The deserted town hall, the empty fountain, as well as the leafy boulevard, the spa itself, a ruined grand hotel and a handful of imposing villas were all that remained of the *terme* because the spring of mineral water had suddenly and for no known reason dried up.

This much Kate and Steve learned from a friendly waiter who served them cappuccino outside the determinedly named Café Fontana, but when it came to the existence of a villa owned, some years ago perhaps, by a contessa he was less informative; he wasn't, he said, a local man, why didn't they ask at the police station, give the lazy so-and-so's something to do for a change?

A young carabiniere, very aware of how handsome he looked in his immaculate uniform, was inclined to be flirtatious, quickly realizing that Steve spoke very little Italian and that the pretty girl spoke it fluently. The waiter, he implied, was a mere peasant who had better get back to his goats. Anyone of any intelligence in Lazzetta knew that Il Campanile belonged to the Conte and Contessa Pilati Castalda. Yes, for many years they had rented it to various visitors, but now they were old they'd come to live there themselves. What, he added, might be the signorina's interest? Kate replied that her uncle and aunt had once been the contessa's tenants. 'Ah!' he said, and reached for a massive tome, blowing the dust off it. 'Now, if the signorina will just give me their name?'

Kate laughed. 'It was *years* ago, fifteen years perhaps—there can't be a record of it.'

'We are highly efficient,' he replied sardonically with a flash of fine teeth. 'Besides, you'd be amazed how few foreign visitors come to Lazzetta Terme.'

'They were called Ackland.' Kate was by now quite intrigued to discover whether Mark and Helen had ever been registered as residents. They had indeed, and only three pages back: two pages, presumably, per decade. Unfortunately he was already closing the book when Kate realized that there was another name written under the two Acklands; it could belong to no one except the mysterious third member of the *ménage-à-trois*, and she had missed it. For a second she was on the point of asking him to reopen the book and show her, but he was now putting it back on its shelf, and also something warned her that too great a show of curiosity might be a mistake. Glancing at her face, he said, 'For further information you'd better apply to the contessa herself.'

Kate's growing excitement might have led her to apply there and then, but Steve now put his foot down firmly. It was six-thirty, and both the lady and her husband were old, they were going to be left alone.

'But,' protested Kate, 'I can ring them, can't I? Make a date to see them tomorrow.'

Steve could hardly object to this, so they went back to the Café Fontana, ordered Campari-sodas, and Kate retired to the telephone. When she returned, the blue-grey eyes were no longer brilliant with excitement. Steve said, 'They won't see us? They're not there?'

She shook her head. 'No, she'd love to see us—any time after nine-thirty tomorrow, they're early risers. We settled on nine-forty-five. She has a thing about the English; I suppose she's old enough to think of us as we used to be.'

'Then what's the matter?'

Kate sat down and took his hand. 'Steve, it's all going so *well*.'

'I don't call dead dogs and setting fire to . . .'

She waved this aside. 'I mean finding Netta. And then Julia. And now, tracing this villa so easily . . .'

Steve laughed. 'But life *isn't* difficult if you go for it—attack it head-on.'

'I'm not sure.'

'Then you should be, you're the living proof of it—we both are.' He picked up the hand and kissed it. 'But *you* have to do the doing. Ninety per cent of people think life is just sitting on their fat bottoms waiting for things to happen. And of course nothing *does* happen, why should it, so they just die without having been alive.'

'I bet Daniel would have a quotation to fit that one.'

'He's a doer all right. How about that cross-country trip in a wheelchair?'

Kate smiled. 'I don't know. When things go smoothly I always feel uneasy—as if something dire is going to happen.'

'Sure. And something dire often does. So what?'

It seemed the most unexpected time and place for certainty to strike her, but she had waited for it a long time and had always known she'd recognize it when it came. She heard her own voice saying, 'I love you, Steve.'

He accepted it as seriously as she had meant it; they stared at each other in silence for a long moment. Then he said, 'I'm going to live up to that one, you see if I don't.'

Late sunlight cast a pattern of leaves on the table and on their clasped hands. The waiter, watching them, smiled at some private memory of his own.

CHAPTER 10

Daniel reckoned, with the aid of British Rail's Southern Region timetable, that if Andrew Howard wanted to be in good time for their twelve o'clock non-meeting at the Savoy, he would certainly catch the nine-twenty from Bournemouth; it only stopped once and was in any case the most comfortable of the morning trains. If he was really so stupid as to drive, he would have to start at about the same time, or even earlier, given the overcrowding of London's ring-road; out of date from the day of its inception. In any event, he could not possibly reappear on the south coast before three in the afternoon, so there was no hurry, and no need for Daniel to call upon Rosemary Howard at an inconvenient hour; eleven a.m. seemed entirely suitable.

It was really Tom Duff's day to look after the Woolpack, but his parents had made no particular arrangement to visit friends or other landlords, and didn't in the least mind swapping their day off with his. When it was time for them to start, Tom appeared looking—as always—scrubbed and immaculate from the top of his neatly shorn fair head to the soles of his new size 12 trainers. Nobody could have called him good-looking, but he had a pleasant country face (his mother often referred to him as 'Farmer Tom'); his other attributes, Daniel had noticed, not without slight jealousy, drew admiring glances from the majority of women; but Tom never seemed to notice this: there wasn't an iota of vanity in his being.

It amused and surprised Daniel that he seemed to be

looking forward to the trip with pleasure, intrigued by its faint air of skulduggery. Could it be that his own weak dependence on this large young man, and his sometimes surprising antics, such as arriving by night in a wheelchair, hands blood-soaked, added another dimension to Tom's life, dedicated to the pub and winter games of rugby? Perhaps.

As they drove along on this fine spring morning he entertained Daniel with some unusually bawdy rugby songs. It was fortunate that he, and Daniel as far as his physical shortcomings allowed, were so full of optimism and energy. They were going to need both.

On that same morning Kate and Steve set out once again for Lazzetta. Lovemaking, and the heady joy of being in each other's company again, filled them to the brim with limitless high spirits and excitement. This, too, was just as well, for they were facing a day which would drain them of all but the last few drops.

They executed the return journey with efficiency, evading the *autostrada* and taking all the right roads so that they arrived at the villa on the dot of 9.45.

Il Campanile, dominated by the tower after which it was named, stood high above the little town, commanding an extraordinary view which included, on this clear day, the distant Gulf of Genoa sparkling into a misty horizon. The villa was not, for a turn-of-the-century building, unduly preposterous, perhaps because much of it was hidden under bougainvillaea and wisteria and, at this time of year, a riot of roses.

The Contessa Pilati Castalda was sitting on the terrace, waiting to welcome them with coffee. She must have been about seventy and clearly had once been a beauty: not the dark, exotic Italian beauty whom Kate and Steve had both been expecting, with fine cheekbones and a narrow nose down which to examine them: no, not that type at all, but a slim, almost gawky, tennis-playing beauty who had once had red-gold hair and still possessed the kind of infectious laugh which bubbled out of her at any thought of pomposity. Yet, in a typically Italian manner, the gawkiness had been turned to grace and the deep blue eyes were too kindly ever to look down her delicate nose at anyone.

Her husband was, by contrast, small and fine-boned with white hair and a luxuriant white moustache; what else he might be they never discovered, for he sat a hundred yards away in the garden, half obscured by a straw hat and wholly absorbed in the watercolour he was painting.

The contessa said, in perfect English, of course, 'This place belonged to my husband's Aunt Editta. Trust *her* to build at a spa with no water! She left it to him, and for years we just ignored it. But then, as we got older and Rome became totally impossible, we decided to come here, and now we love it and feel as if we'd lived here all our lives. Our friends think us *most* eccentric!' And a freshet of that beguiling laughter made her look a girl again.

She asked tenderly after England, and had fond memories of London which, she confessed, she had not visited for many years, so that the city of which she spoke bore no relation to the dirty, mismanaged, grasping tourist trap of the present day. It was difficult to answer her questions without destroying those memories, but she was too intelligent not to see through their evasions and said with a sigh, 'Sometimes I'm glad to be old. Rome, London, Paris—one knew them when they were their own individual selves.'

She was perhaps relieved to turn to the Acklands whom she recalled very clearly. The count had always insisted that his wife should interview, in person, the people to whom they had occasionally rented Il Campanile. Some, she added, with no trace of arrogance, were truly impossible and had to be discouraged; but the Acklands had been acceptable, even though one understood that he was a bit of a *mauvais garçon*—she'd heard some very odd stories about him. Well, to be frank, about both of them. 'But I think,' she added, saving Kate an infinity of artful leading questions, 'that the very fact of their friend being so ill . . . It was hardly a time for . . . misbehaviour, was it?'

So here, once again, but with no self-satisfied carabiniere standing guard over it, they were at last confronting the *ménage-à-trois*. It didn't seem to be quite the kind which Rosemary Howard, or indeed Julia, had imagined.

'Was he . . . ill when they came here?'

'Oh yes. I never saw him, mind you, it was none of my business. I think your aunt in particular was very fond of him. Perhaps her husband too, because . . . Well, they could neither of them bear to stay here very long after he was dead.'

Kate caught Steve's eye and knew that he, like her, was appreciating this alternative, and typically kind-hearted, explanation of the Ackland's flight from Lazzetta. Yet the contessa had not known them and Julia had; therefore her diagnosis of unease and even fear seemed to ring more true than the older woman's generous interpretation. She added, 'They were here such a short time too—a month, perhaps a little more.'

'Is that all?' Kate was yet again surprised by the brevity of the stay; had they never settled anywhere for more than a few weeks? The contessa gestured. 'To tell you the truth, I'm not absolutely sure how long they stayed, it may have been less than a month. They didn't move in until some time after they'd started paying the rent. Rather a wasteful way to carry on.'

Despite the open—and open-air—façade which she presented to the world, she was also a knowledgeable and sophisticated woman who had spent much of her life in Rome, that snakepit of intrigue and scandal, and the look she now turned on the young English couple made it quite clear that she wondered *why* they were in pursuit of the past: she was far too well-mannered to ask directly, but said, 'If you want more details about the poor man you could always go and see Dr Montieri. The son has taken over the practice—we find him most satisfactory—but the father would have treated Mr . . . What *was* his name?' She called out to her husband, 'Dominico? What was the name of the Acklands' friend who died?'

Without looking up from his painting he called back in a thin, carrying voice, 'Camden, my dear, Edward Camden.'

She shook her head in admiration. 'Such a memory, mine went years ago! As I was saying, Leonardo Montieri would have treated Mr Camden. I'm sure he'd be delighted to see you. We all love Lazzetta but we all have to admit that nothing ever happens.' Again the youthful laugh.

Steve broke his silence by saying, 'We were told he's buried here.'

'Yes, in our little cemetery above the town—you passed it on your way up the hill. I suppose that means he was a Catholic, though the Church can sometimes be quite civilized about such things.'

Kate, who now felt that explanation was long overdue, said, 'You must think we're being very inquisitive, but Uncle Mark and Aunt Helen have always been . . . you know, one of the mysteries of our family . . .'

'All families have them. My great-grandfather was said to have been a dwarf who was never allowed to leave his home. So you're pursuing a mystery.'

'As you just said, Uncle Mark had a terrible reputation when he was a young man. Of course, he refuses to talk about it now, so . . . Well, you can understand why I'm curious.'

'The young should always be curious.' She knew, as well as Kate did, that nothing had been explained but that a necessary convention had been observed. This gave the girl courage to say, 'I think they were in Italy for quite a long time, but I've no idea where they were before they came here.'

'Oh, one heard of his ... exploits from time to time over the years. In Rome, of course. Venice, Naples. The Fabrianis took him to court, I can't remember what for. I think they'd been living near Verona before they came to Lazzetta.'

Realizing that she was teetering on the brink of bad manners, and trusting that youth would excuse her, Kate asked, 'Still with this Edward Camden?'

The contessa's deep blue eyes gave her the nearest they could achieve to a sharp glance. 'One gathers he went everywhere with them.' Her tone made it clear that she had now gone as far as she was prepared to go—at least on such short acquaintance—and to prove it she added, 'My dear, I think you should be careful whom you talk to about such things. Not everyone is circumspect.'

'I'm sorry.' Kate produced her most innocent smile. 'Of course, I'm taking advantage of the fact that you aren't "everyone", or I wouldn't have dared question you like this. I'm a shameless girl of my generation.'

The laugh came bubbling up. 'You don't strike me as shameless, but you're certainly of your generation; who isn't?' She turned to Steve. 'Whereas you, my young friend, are most undemanding.'

'Ah,' said Steve, 'that's because I know Kate will demand quite enough without my help.'

'Quite enough! But all the same it was a pleasure talking to you.'

When they were nearly at their car she called out after them, 'You'd better visit Dr Montieri this morning, we old people are given to extended siestas.'

Thus warned, they drove back towards the town but,

since it was still only a few minutes after eleven, turned off the road to take a quick look at the cemetery which was placed, in the Italian manner, well away from Lazzetta on a small plateau: little more than another, wider terrace but not for the planting of olives or vines. There were a few grandiose monuments, dating from before the drying up of the waters, and many of those curious Italian filing cabinets for the dead, piled one upon the other in deep niches hollowed from the rock. EDWARD LIFFORD CAMDEN lay to one side of the terrace where brambles tended to intrude (perhaps he had not after all been a Catholic and was only here on sufferance): a plain headstone, giving his name, dates of birth and death, and nothing else. He had been thirty-five when he died.

Gazing at the stone, Kate quoted the contessa: 'One gathers he went everywhere with them.'

Steve nodded. 'There was *something* she wasn't saying. Maybe Julia was right, and he *was* your Aunt Helen's lover. Or your Uncle Mark's.'

'I never heard that Mark went in for that kind of thing.'

'In his wild, wild youth?'

'Oh God, who knows? What's wrong with his being Helen's lover anyway?'

'I get the feeling Mark wouldn't have put up with it.'

'No, I don't think he would. So perhaps they were . . . you know, just close friends, just three people who liked travelling together.'

'Perhaps. Why not?'

But the explanation satisfied neither of them, and rendered them both silent, thinking. Eventually Kate said, 'I was really surprised they only stayed here a few weeks.'

'You showed it. And I wonder why they didn't go there right away—why rent the place and not use it? Like gangsters with a hide-out.'

'I've always held they had a very good reason for

everything they did. But all this apparently pointless movement! A few weeks here, even less in La Spezia, I'm sure Julia was telling the truth. *Were* they escaping from something, as she said, and if so, what?'

Getting no answer, she turned and found Steve rubbing his chin and regarding her intently.

'What's the matter?'

'Oh . . . nothing. I was thinking how nice it would be to go back to the hotel and go to bed.'

'You call that nothing!' She laughed and leaned into his arms and they embraced among the silent dead and the noisy cicadas, with the remains of Edward Lifford Camden at their feet.

Kate said, 'If we don't see the doctor before lunch we'll be sitting on his doorstep twiddling our thumbs until three or four o'clock.'

On one side of Lazzetta's spacious *piazza* was a flight of stone steps, flanked by balustrades with two pairs of handsome cast-iron lamps at top and bottom. This had been designed as the main approach, by foot, to the spa itself, but was now merely a short-cut to a number of residential streets on the higher slopes of the town. The Doctors Montieri, father and son, lived in one of these streets, so Steve parked the rented Fiat in the square, and he and Kate climbed the ornate steps hand in hand. At the top they paused, looking back at the *piazza*, the carabinieri headquarters immediately opposite, town hall to the left, shady tree-lined boulevard to the right; in fact, most of Lazzetta lay at their feet.

They would have recognized Number 20, Via Cavour without reading the number, because a man who could only have been Dr Montieri Junior was just coming out of it holding a doctor's bag. The house was a choice example of *terme* architecture, tastefully decorated with terracotta plaques of a vaguely Egyptian provenance. Young Dr Montieri was tall and thin, in his late thirties, with a single streak of white hair emphasizing an otherwise black widow's peak. His dark eyes behind dark horn-rimmed glasses seemed to become uneasy as soon as he heard the purpose of their visit. Perhaps he was even considering excuses for his father's absence, because there was a pause when Kate had finished speaking. But eventually he shrugged and said, 'He's very busy on his book, but . . . I can ask him.' They followed him into a dark hall lit by a single stained-glass window: a lotus design, naturally.

There was then a hiatus, and the faint mumble of male voices in the distance. A woman joined in, protesting by the sound of it. Steve glanced at Kate and raised his eyebrows.

Montieri Junior reappeared, hurrying now like the White Rabbit and consulting his watch. He said, 'Father will be with you in a moment. Please.' And he ushered them into a waiting-room which must have been redecorated since the turn of the century but managed to give the impression that it had not. There was even an aspidistra obscuring the fireplace.

Leonardo Montieri, when he silently manifested himself (he was wearing patent-leather slippers) was as tall as his son, with the beautiful pure white hair which is only granted to dark, usually Mediterranean men. *His* glasses, however, had gold frames and were worn low on the nose so that he could look over them.

He said, 'I was tempted to tell some stupid lie, via my son, and not to see you. But then I thought, "Leonardo Montieri, you have become an old fool. For years and years you have been expecting somebody to ask questions about Edward Camden, and now that they're here you run away!" So . . .' He gestured with long, beautiful fingers. 'Here I am. You are his relatives?'

'No, but the Acklands who were with him up at Il Campanile, they are my uncle and aunt.'

'Indeed. I did not find them *simpatico*. But I was angry with them.'

'Why angry?'

He examined her at length over the gold rims, and motioned them both to sit down. They sat on horsehair, hard and ample enough to support a bustle, if not a crinoline.

'I should perhaps explain that I'd had problems with some of the contessa's previous tenants. Americans. One of them became extremely ill, and neither she nor her friends improved matters by withholding information. I suspected she'd had an abortion but she denied it and was abusive when I found out myself by the usual procedures. It didn't seem to have occurred to her, or her friends, that she might have died.'

'Stupid!' said Steve.

'There are vast numbers of stupid people in the world, and the Pilati Castalda seem to choose a high proportion of them as tenants. In the days before they came to live there themselves, I was wary of Il Campanile—so I'm sure you'll forgive me, signorina, if I ask you what your interest is in Edward Camden's death?'

'You may not forgive *me*, Doctor, if I tell you it's a kind of curiosity.'

He shook his head. 'Any doctor who finds curiosity objectionable is a fool: it's the foundation of our profession.'

'My uncle and aunt are a mystery in my family, I want to know about them.' It had worked with the contessa, why shouldn't it work with the doctor?

'So your interest is in them rather than in Mr Camden?'

'In both. I think they were . . . interdependent.'

'You speak excellent Italian. Yes, I too think they were

interdependent.' He looked at Steve. 'And you, signore—you also speak my language?'

'Very little, but I can understand it.'

Dr Montieri nodded absently, his thoughts in the past. 'I was angry with your uncle and aunt because they did not *immediately* report Mr Camden's condition to me on their arrival. Later they told me that illness had made him very difficult, he became angry for no reason, and they could see how much worse anger made him, so they tried to keep him as calm as possible. He also hated doctors. He even . . . Well, many patients say it, not all mean it—he claimed he wanted to die, said he was sick to death of being sick. I have always remembered that phrase.'

'It had been going on for a long time.'

'Yes, on and off, sometimes better, sometimes worse. But when I saw him it had reached its terminal stages, and he was in a coma.'

'What was it?'

'You would call it double pneumonia. Of course, I at once gave him the wonder-drug of that time, an oral form of penicillin. I also gave him a massive injection. Neither effected any improvement in his condition.'

Steve said, in slow and correct Italian, 'He was too ill for treatment?'

'He was extremely ill, but I was surprised to find no improvement after I'd administered the drugs. In answer to your question—yes, that's what I told myself and the Acklands. "You called me too late, he was too far gone."'

He rested his elbows on his knees and put his face in his hands for a moment; then drew them both back over his hair, and sat up straight again. The young man and woman thought it an odd, overly dramatic gesture, but not when they heard what he had to say next.

'Since no one, not one relative, has ever come here to see me, it is . . . something of a relief to speak of this matter.'

'He died.'

'Oh yes, signorina, he died, that was inevitable. I refer to another matter. With Mr and Mrs Ackland, Edward Camden had travelled widely, all over Europe and into Asia Minor. Among many, many other places where they spent some time was the city of Tangier. It is a place which has an unfortunate effect on certain Anglo-Saxons—we Southerners are . . . less susceptible. Anyway, according to your uncle, who was always very frank with me, Mr Camden had already been drinking too much. He then took to khif, perhaps other drugs. But I should make it clear that there were no physical signs of heroin, or any other substance, having been intravenously injected. He also took to having sexual intercourse with a wide variety of the youngsters who ply for trade in Tangier. Your uncle said that he developed a preference for boys, all of them Arab or . . . from more southern parts of Africa. His various illnesses began shortly after this time.'

Kate said, 'Oh!' and put a hand up to her mouth. Steve shook his head and sighed.

'You're quick, both of you. But you're young and you live *now*. Don't forget I'm speaking of a time before such a condition had become, alas, commonplace.'

'And he didn't react to the latest drugs.'

'Correct. Only later, two or three years later when information was being released from the United States did I suspect that I had attended an early European case of the HIV virus.'

'Poor man!'

'I have the greatest sympathy for many sufferers, but little for Mr Camden—a man who sleeps with trash will climb out of bed with trash adhering to him. I eventually discovered the whereabouts of Mr and Mrs Ackland and wrote to them in Corsica advising them to submit to tests. I was particularly worried about your aunt since there were tales . . . gossip, one imagines . . . It was said that she and Mr Camden had once been lovers. I received no answer.'

He paused; then shrugged and asked, 'Your uncle and aunt are alive and well?'

'Yes.'

'Then that's my answer for which I thank you. Though I'm not surprised, the risks are greatly exaggerated. Needless to say, I didn't mention my suspicions to anyone else—there was no point, the man had long ago been buried.'

'There were no . . . awkward questions about his death?'

'No, signorina. Since I'm medical consultant to . . . the Coroner, I think you call him . . .'

'Yes, we do.'

'. . . my colleagues accepted my diagnosis, which was perfectly correct as far as it went. The direct cause of Mr Camden's death *was* undoubtedly a severe attack of double pneumonia.'

They walked away from the doctor's house in silence and deep thought. After a moment Steve glanced at her. 'It seems to fit, doesn't it?'

'With what? The contessa's story?'

'And Julia's. They must have been very fond of Edward Camden, both of them. They seem to have stuck by him through thick and thin.'

'No.' She was decisive. 'I can't see Mark and Helen being that loyal to anyone. Unless there was a damn good reason.'

They had reached the top of the steps. Steve said, 'People change. It was a long time ago, and perhaps in those days they weren't so—'

'*Oh my God!*' Kate had jerked herself away from him, and was now pressed flat between one of the cast-iron lamps and a dusty oleander. Her face was white, the beautiful eyes wide with shock. He stared at her, amazed.

'Look . . . at the police station.'

Steve looked. A car marked 'Carabinieri' had drawn up in front of it and two men were getting out: one slim, a uniformed lieutenant, the other larger, in civilian clothes.

Kate's voice was dry, choked: 'The big man—it's Uncle Mark.'

CHAPTER 11

Daniel had suspected, at their first and only meeting, that Rosemary Howard didn't altogether enjoy the restraints imposed upon her by her son. Her manner and appearance at this second visit confirmed the suspicion. She had taken great trouble with her face, and somebody had done the same for her hair. She looked sprightly, even excited, like a small girl excused school.

Neither she nor her somewhat starchy nurse were at pains to hide their feelings. The latter welcomed him with, 'I'm so glad you came back. A change of company does her all the good in the world.' And Mrs Howard herself elaborated with a flash of the bright blue eyes, by adding, 'I always like it when Andrew goes to London. I'm sorry he was so rude to you the other day—I thought we'd have a little treat to make up for it.'

The treat, brought in by the nurse who lingered to take a glass with them, was champagne, a vintage Bollinger, and exactly what any sensible person who could afford it would enjoy at eleven o'clock in the morning. Would it also, Daniel wondered, loosen the old lady's tongue a little? She would never divulge everything, but on coming near her, now as before, he was quite sure that all kinds of odds and ends of information lay within his grasp, and that one or more of them, unconnected as far as she was concerned, could link together and complete the broken chain of reasoning in his own mind.

However, once the nurse had withdrawn she surprised him by smiling at him over her glass and saying, 'I never asked before, but I've been wondering ever since you were here with your sister—just *why* are you so interested in the past, in that old letter of mine?'

Like Kate, Daniel always had a variety of excuses on the tip of his tongue, but he decided that in her present highly lucid condition the truth, or part of it, might provide a beneficial shock. 'Did it never strike you as odd that so soon after she'd told you of her suspicions and the steps she proposed to take, she fell downstairs and was killed?'

The old woman nodded and put a hand up to her chest in a gesture which he remembered. 'Yes, of course it did. That's why I was . . . so terribly relieved when you told me how the letter had fallen behind some panelling and been lost.'

In for a penny, in for a pound, Daniel said, 'You mean you were afraid Mark might see it.'

'Yes. Though I didn't mention his name in it, did I?'

'No.'

'All the same, if what she said was true, he would have realized she had . . . suspicions about him.'

'Perhaps he realized anyway.'

'I've often wondered. But at least I . . . I wasn't in any way responsible, was I?'

'No, you weren't.'

She gave him one of her bright bird-like glances. 'This is a very *odd* conversation.'

Since they had just agreed, though not in so many words, that Mark Ackland might possibly have killed his mother, Daniel was thinking the same. He raised his glass. 'Must be your beautiful champagne.'

'It *is* good, isn't it? My husband's favourite.'

'Odd or not, I was only answering your question. Kate and I are interested because we're pretty sure Grandmother didn't die by accident. We'd like to know the truth.'

'I've always found the truth rather dangerous myself.'

'Yes, it is.' He leaned forward. 'Mrs Howard, when we were here before, my sister asked you outright what it was Grandmother had said to you. She's like that, very outspoken . . .'

'Just like dear Lydia.'

'I didn't think it was a sensible question—so I wasn't a bit surprised when you evaded it.'

'You're an observant young man. And surely I told you how strangely she was talking?'

'Yes, you did. But she was always like that when she was angry.'

'Oh, but I'd never seen her so . . . so uncontrolled. I really was very worried.'

Daniel kept quiet and held his breath. He had at least guided her back into the past, and hoped that her memories would now take over.

'I even asked that nice girl who worked for her whether she'd been in this condition for long. I mean, I had an awful feeling she ought to be in a home. Most of it was nonsense, pure nonsense.'

She nodded to herself and fell silent. Daniel had to nudge her again: 'In what way?'

'My dear, she was saying that Mark shouldn't have stayed away all that time, never even coming back to see her. Heavens above!' She gestured with her empty glass. 'Didn't she throw him out of England in the first place? She didn't *want* him to come and see her, she wouldn't have spoken to him if he had—and I told her as much. So then she lost her temper with me and called me a coward. As if that had anything to do with it!'

Daniel leaned forward and topped up both their glasses.

She nodded thanks, but was now completely caught up in that fraught weekend. 'And then she went on and on about Helen. I must say I never *liked* Helen, too pleased with herself by half, but it wasn't "all her fault", and that's what Lydia kept saying—"Of course, it's all Helen's fault." Well, it wasn't, and I told her so. Mark was an impossible man, and Helen coped with him remarkably well. But Lydia wasn't having any of that, oh no! Helen had only married Mark for the money, because he was heir to Longwater. That was what she wanted, and come hell or high water that was what she intended to get.'

'But,' said Daniel, genuinely puzzled, 'Helen had already *got* Longwater years before.'

'I told you—she simply wasn't making sense. And then she kept going back to that time in Italy. So long ago, I couldn't see how it had anything to do with it. I mean, we all knew—at least I did—about his bad behaviour. Bad! It must have been appalling if even Gerald and I heard about it from our own Italian friends—by no means members of the "jet-set" as I believe it was called in those days.'

'You said there was a law-suit.'

'More than one, I imagine. And then he fell or jumped out of that window in Venice, didn't he? Or perhaps somebody pushed him. Anyway he landed in a cobbled yard, not a canal.'

'News to me.'

'Oh yes. Broke his leg—badly. They thought he might lose it, but some clever Italian surgeon patched it up with a metal plate or something—he still limps a bit, doesn't he?' She took a mouthful of Bollinger. 'We gathered that Helen had her moments too.'

'Lovers?'

'That was the story. Lots of men wanted her to leave him and marry them.' But, thought Daniel to himself,

Helen wanted Longwater and the fortune which went with it, and 'come hell or high water that was what she intended to get'. Mm!

'But you see,' Rosemary was now saying, 'they went too far, those kind of people always do. The whole thing turned sour on them.'

'The, er . . . jet-set wasn't amused any more.'

'To put it mildly. They'd outstayed their welcome, all their welcomes. So they lost most of their so-called friends—acquaintances really.'

'And that night Grandmother kept going back to this?'

'*Harped* on it. Quite bewildering!' Frowning, she sipped her champagne, and then added more thoughtfully: 'I think one of the reasons I couldn't understand what she was driving at was that she didn't *want* me to understand. She did and she didn't, do you know what I mean?'

'Perfectly.'

'I'll tell you another thing—she never really trusted me, not completely. She often used to say I was a bit silly. Well, compared to her I probably was. She thought I chattered too much without forethought. I expect I'm doing it right now, but I don't care any more.'

'You're saying that even if she'd really wanted to tell you what was on her mind she might have . . . pulled back from it.'

'You're a bright boy, that's just what I mean.'

'She was like that with everybody—about the family most of all.'

'Oh heavens, the *family*! I know you'll forgive me for saying this, dear, even if you're an Ackland yourself, but quite frankly your blood isn't that special; my own family's a lot more aristocratic, and I told her so.'

'Brave of you.'

'She didn't like it.'

'I bet she didn't.'

The old woman withdrew her eyes from the past which seemed to lie outside the windows somewhere above the English Channel, and looked at him directly. 'Can you understand how she was talking a kind of sense which was also nonsense?'

'And then getting angry because one couldn't understand.'

'Yes, yes. How well you knew her.'

'She used to do it to me even when I was a little boy. But children are pretty quick, I learned how to read between the lines.'

'I never did. And after a while I got so angry with her I didn't care—that night was no exception. But I shouldn't have been angry, I'd never seen her so ... yes, so wild, and I'd known her for over thirty-five years. I'll tell you how concerned I was—when I heard she might have thrown herself down those stairs, done away with herself, I could almost believe it. And that's a shocking thing to admit about an old and dearly loved friend.'

'You thought she was that ... unhinged?'

'Yes, I did.'

'And of course, it's why you advised her to keep her mouth shut. You said in your letter, people would just dismiss her as a batty old woman.'

'Yes, and I was right, they would have done.'

'Yet Sally, the companion, says she was as bright as a button up to the day she died.'

'That's as may be ... Yes, why don't we finish the bottle? That's as may be, my dear. She died ... was it five days later? All *I'm* saying is that on the evening I'm telling you about she was ... really, out of her mind.'

'With anger?'

'Partly. Or perhaps entirely, she had a terrible temper.'

'She certainly had.'

Rosemary Howard studied him for a moment in silence.

'You're both young, you and your sister. I . . . don't expect you to take my advice any more than Lydia did. She called me a coward. Perhaps I am.' Her head fell suddenly against the back of the chair. 'Oh dear, I'm going to drop off. Age is boring, but . . . I did enjoy the champagne.' A veiled glance from the blue eyes. 'Please take care. Better to be a . . . a coward and alive than . . . Lydia wouldn't have agreed, would she?'

Daniel took her frail, cold hand and pressed it. 'Thank you, Mrs Howard, thank you very much.'

She smiled faintly. And then snored.

He turned out of her room and said goodbye to the buxom nurse who was reading a newspaper in the kitchen; once more he noted what different women both she and her patient were when the dreaded Andrew was absent. Before returning to Tom and the Land-Rover he walked for a few minutes among the pines; stood staring at children running along the beach, but without seeing them, his mind elsewhere.

At their first meeting he had suspected that the old lady was being purposely misleading, out of loyalty to her old friend or out of fear. This time she had spoken more openly; had perhaps told him all she knew insofar as she understood it. He had learned a lot of things, but nothing which struck him with the lightning-flash of revelation. He hadn't even realized until now how much he'd been looking forward to such a flash. Instead of which he felt baulked, deflated, and without any good reason.

Such null reactions were rare in his life; they irritated him, and it was an irritated face which Tom, looking up over an old James Bond paperback, saw emerging from among the trees.

Daniel clambered into the passenger seat and sat there, inert, staring straight ahead.

Tom ventured, 'No good?'

'I don't know.'

Tom didn't think he'd ever heard his brainy friend say 'I don't know'. Never before; it was unnerving. Eyeing the woebegone expression, he felt great sympathy, but was entirely unable to find words that could express it. This was nothing new; he wasn't much good with words. After a time he asked, 'Where do we go now?'

Daniel shrugged. 'Home, I suppose. Stop at some pub on the way for a bite and a beer.'

His mind seemed to be marooned in an impenetrable fog; but after they'd driven a couple of miles he thought he detected a slight shifting of the murk, and for a moment he almost caught a glimpse of an interesting shape before visibility again receded to zero.

After six or seven miles he became convinced that there was in fact something there, it wasn't pure imagination or wishful thinking. He forced his retentive memory to rerun the entire conversation over the bottle of superior champagne, starting with their tacit and surprised realization that they could both suspect Mark of having killed his mother; passing over the tangle of uncertainties and repetitions which had followed; passing over the unsurprising fact that Grandmother Lydia had not altogether trusted her old friend (whom *did* she altogether trust?) and thought her a tittle-tattle; ending with Rosemary's warning: 'Please take care. Better to be a coward and alive than . . . Lydia wouldn't have agreed, would she?'

He found no clue. The shape in his fogged brain still lurked just out of sight. He was sullen and silent, sagging into himself. Tom, upright, sunny and ebullient, drove carefully and sometimes sang softly in his pleasing baritone.

The fog lifted with breathtaking suddenness in the middle of their gloomy snack at the Pear Tree in Brocklebank; Daniel let out a gasp, dropped his hunk of game pie into Tom's pint of beer, upset his own glass all over the table, and turned with wide, wild eyes. 'Dear Jesus Christ, *of course*!' No longer sullen, his face was alight, on fire.

Tom nodded, pleased; this was more like the old Daniel. Pity about his pint!

'What did she *say*? Oh God, what was it, what was it?'

Tom stared, smiling; was in fact way ahead of him; his understanding was acute, if normally unexpressed. 'You want to go back and ask her, right?'

'Tom, I *must*!'

The big young man glanced at the watch on his brawny wrist. 'What if your favourite lawyer comes home from London fighting mad?'

'It's a risk we've got to take. Come on!'

'Three minutes. I'm getting another pint, it was a drop of all right. How about you?'

'Hell, no! I mean, thanks, Tom—we've got to go.'

'Three minutes.' In fact he sank his pint in one, and by the end of three they'd embarked on the return journey to Bournemouth; Tom driving fast, Daniel thinking furiously and occasionally muttering under his breath.

There was no sign of the maroon Mercedes outside The Pines, but neither was there any longer a sense of happy relaxation within. The nurse's face froze in horror when she saw who the visitor was. Apparently Andrew Howard had called from London 'in a terrible state', asking if Mr Daniel Ackland had paid a call. On hearing that he indeed had ('I couldn't lie to him—he's a lawyer, he always finds out anyway') he had been speechless with fury; she was sure that this was the end of her present job—such a nice job too, and they got on so well together, she and Mrs Howard, when *he* wasn't around.

Tom, who had stayed with the Land-Rover, could see that there was some kind of altercation in progress and came over to join them at the door. Daniel was saying,

'I *must* speak to her again, only for a few minutes. Five minutes.'

'No, no! Please go away. She's having her afternoon rest, she's asleep.'

'I'm not asleep,' came Rosemary's voice, very alert. 'What's going on? Who is it?'

Daniel laid a hand on the nurse's arm and said, 'Tom here will look after you if Andrew appears.' And, while she was turning to bestow the usual glance of feminine appreciation upon Tom's size and strength, he slipped past her, across the hall and into Mrs Howard's room. She was lying on the bed, propped against many pillows, and the blue eyes were bright. 'Oh, it's you again, dear. How nice! A bit too early for tea, I'm afraid.'

'I only want to clarify one thing, one small thing.'

'You played a naughty trick on my son, didn't you?'

'I'm sorry.'

'Do him good, he's far too bossy. What do you want to ask me?'

Daniel tried to compose himself. It was essential that there should be no leading questions; the information must come directly from her. 'When you and Grandmother were arguing about family . . .'

'All that silly snobbishness!'

'I agree. Can you remember *exactly* what you both said?' He could almost feel Andrew thundering towards them, all guns blazing, but managed to add, 'Take your time.'

'Well now, let me see . . .' The pause was endless. 'She was boasting about the Acklands, and by that time I was absolutely fed up, we'd been at it for hours, I was exhausted. I said something like, "Lydia, we've done the family over and over again—and anyway the Acklands aren't all that well-bred." I said, "To be honest, my own family's a lot more aristocratic." And she said, "Oh Rosemary, don't be such a nitwit, I'm talking about the blood . . ."' She looked up at him sharply. 'No, wait a minute! She'd got back on to Mark cheating your father, and she said, "But there *is* proof, it's in the blood," and it was *then* I said my family was more aristocratic than hers, and she lost her temper and told me I was a damn fool . . .'

At this moment sudden and unmistakable noises-off betokened the arrival of her son.

Daniel, eyes shining, grasped her cool hand and said, 'Thank you, oh *thank* you!'

'But I've hardly told you . . .'

'You,' shouted Andrew Howard from the door, 'are going to find yourself in a court of law.'

Daniel swung around as fast as his crutches would allow. 'You think so.'

'I damn well know it.'

'Good. Because then *you* can explain what happened when you went to see my grandmother three days before she was killed on that staircase.'

Andrew's stupefaction was momentary but unmistakable. 'She wanted to consult me on a family matter. At my mother's recommendation.'

'Yes. And she changed her mind, didn't she? She saw right through you and she didn't trust what she saw—I don't blame her.'

'Unjustifiable nonsense!'

'That's why you were so keen to get your grubby hands on the letter—she didn't trust you and she shut up like a clam. But that didn't stop you running over to Longwater House there and then, telling my Uncle Mark she intended to cause trouble.'

'I'll have you for slander, defamation . . .' He pointed at the gaping nurse. 'I have witnesses.'

Daniel went closer to him, face very pale. 'Slander, my foot! This is going to be a trial for murder and you're going to be an accessory after the fact!'

Master Howard's mouth opened. No sound emerged. Then he lunged forward, fist raised. The nurse screamed. Tom, moving with the speed which so distinguished him on the rugby field, grabbed the plump lawyer from behind with both arms and lifted him clear off the floor. Andrew kicked out backwards, and Tom, by way of reprisal, raised one knee and thumped him hard in the groin. Andrew howled. Tom released him and pushed him backwards on to a sofa where he lay gasping like a stranded fish.

Rosemary Howard, suddenly strident, said, 'Andrew, can this be true? Did you really go over to Longwater and betray Lydia's confidences?'

'Of course not.'

'You're lying, dear. I told you—I remember telling you before you went to Woodman's. The strictest confidence. Lydia Ackland was my best friend.'

'It's nothing to do with you, Mother.'

The pale blue eyes blazed for a moment. 'It'll be something to do with me if I change my will and leave it all to World Wildlife.' She waved at Daniel as he hobbled out of the door, Tom bringing up the rear. The last they heard was her voice, not at all the voice of a helpless invalid, saying, 'You'd better tell me the truth, my boy, or you may regret it.'

Daniel, heading for the Land-Rover, said, 'Thanks, Tom. My God, if he'd hit me I'd have gone down like a ninepin—he'd probably have kicked me to death.'

'Pleasure's mine. He's a real sod, that one!' He glanced at Daniel's face and smiled. 'Got what you wanted, didn't you? Written all over you.'

'I'll say! But why the hell didn't I see it before? It was there all the time, staring me in the face. I've got to tell Kate.'

CHAPTER 12

At about the same time of the afternoon on that same day, a badly shaken Kate, and Steve at his most alert, had waited until her Uncle Mark, with the lieutenant of the carabinieri, had turned into Lazzetta's police station; then they had beaten a hasty retreat around the corner and back into the Via Cavour where Dr Montieri lived and where they were out of sight from the *piazza*.

'Well, well,' said Steve. 'Uncle's hand on the copper's shoulder. Thick as thieves, you might say.'

Kate was still trembling. 'But how did he know . . . ?'

'Oh come *on*, love! You gave your name to that beautiful hunk last night, right there in the police station.'

'But . . . to get here so quickly!'

'Proves a couple of things, doesn't it? One—he's got friends in the carabinieri, and someone's been keeping an eye open on his behalf . . .'

'All this time?'

'Sure, that's what money's for. And two—something very weird *did* happen in this town all those years ago.'

She nodded, staring at him, trying to pull herself together.

'In any case, he had a lot of warning. You were at Cortiano—you were on the trail and you disappeared. He was probably putting two and two together long before anyone told him you'd got here. Right?'

Kate nodded again.

'The thing is, what do we do now?'

'Blow this place for a start.'

Steve shook his head. 'Why?'

'Oh God!' She ran a hand through her hair. 'I don't

know. Seeing him like that . . . Pure panic, I suppose.'

'The whole point of the exercise is to find out what went on here. His turning up like this is part of it. So somehow we've got to keep an eye on him. He'll lead us straight to it, Kate, he hasn't come here just to keep us company, he's come to *do* something.'

She understood what Françoise had meant about men: 'They think practically. We can, but we tend not to.'

He continued, 'The vital thing is that Uncle mustn't see *you*. He can't recognize me, that gives us room for manoeuvre.'

She found this quiet pragmatism most soothing and thanked God for his presence. Left to her own devices she'd by now be driving like a bat out of hell down the steep road to San Pietro Vara: losing the trail just when it promised to lead somewhere.

Watching her with his dark steady eyes, he added, 'There's only one thing—nobody knows where we are, that could be dangerous if things get rough.'

'Rough?'

'He *is* in cahoots with the carabinieri.' He nodded to himself and took her arm, leading her quickly back to Dr Montieri's house where he marched up the steps and rang the bell.

'What are you doing?'

'You're going to do the doing—call your brother.'

'But we can't just walk into someone's . . .'

Dr Montieri Senior himself opened the door. Kate stared at him. Steve said, 'Go on, love, tell him we could be in danger.'

It was obviously not the kind of situation to which the old doctor was accustomed but he didn't ask any of the questions which might have been expected. Doctors are used to emergencies; unnecessary questions can waste time and jeopardize lives. And perhaps the contessa had been right: they all loved Lazzetta but had to admit that nothing ever happened. Here was a little drama to brighten the day. Montieri merely said, 'The telephone is rather expensive. You won't mind if the exchange advises us of the cost. I will leave you.'

'No, please. It doesn't matter, and I . . . I may need help getting the number.'

But no amount of help could have achieved that; the operator was sorry, all lines to England were engaged, and many subscribers were waiting.

Steve said, 'Forget England. Call Françoise and ask her to pass the message to your brother as soon as possible.'

It seemed to take an infinity, but in the end Kate was connected to Corsica, to Bastia, to the Café l'Oasis, to Françoise. She said, 'We're in trouble and I can't get through to my brother in England . . .'

The cool, unfazed voice asked, 'What is his number? Good, I have that. And the message?'

Steve was delighted to see that Kate had got over her shock and was again the girl who ran an extremely successful hotel. 'Four things, Françoise. One—we're at Lazzetta, inland from Sestri Levante. Two—Mark Ackland has just arrived, and he's got friends in the carabinieri. Therefore, three—we could be in danger. Four—the name of the other man in the *ménage-à-trois* was Edward Camden. OK?'

Françoise repeated the message and asked if they were still registered at the Hotel Bobbio in La Spezia.

'Yes, but I don't think we'll be going back there just yet.'

'I'll call Monsieur Daniel immediately. If he's not there, may I dictate your message, are the people reliable?'

'Yes, absolutely. Thank you, Françoise. We both send our love.'

Steve leaned over and kissed her cheek. 'That's more like my girl.'

'Now what?'

'Now we wait to find out how much we owe Dr Montieri.'

The old man's only comment on all this was to shake his head and say, 'I'm sorry to hear that Signor Ackland is back in Lazzetta. He is not *simpatico*.'

When they'd left 20, Via Cavour for the second time that day, Steve said, 'I wonder if Uncle's still in there with the carabinieri.' They didn't have to go as far as the steps to see that the car had not moved from in front of the police station. 'Do you suppose I could find out anything?'

'How d'you mean?'

'By going in there. With some cock-and-bull story about . . . I don't know, being robbed.'

'But as soon as they hear an English voice, they'll suspect . . .'

'*Nein, nein. Können Sie mir helfen? Ich habe mein Kamera verloren.*'

Kate now found that she could even laugh. 'Your accent's appalling.'

'They won't speak German anyway.'

'If the beautiful hulk's there he'll recognize you.'

'He won't be there—not the same duty two days running, all police stations work a rota.'

'What about me?'

'Café Fontana. It's quite dark in that inner room. Put your scarf over your head, put your dark glasses on your pretty nose; let's go.' He was far from sure that the gambit would pay off, and there was no guarantee that Mark Ackland hadn't departed with his friend the lieutenant; but he felt it was worth trying: felt very strongly that if they didn't follow up at once, *do* something, however quirky, the game would slip away from them. Kate, he was glad to say, seemed to agree.

They gave the *piazza* a wide berth and approached the café via a side alley and the main boulevard. He left her in the Edwardian gloom of the *salone* and went straight to the police station; the car still stood outside it, and, as he entered, trying to look like an outraged German, he realized that his old friend Luck, after some irrational behaviour in the recent past, might once again be on his side. A door to the right of the entrance was ajar, and through the gap he caught a glimpse of Mark Ackland's broad back. He couldn't hear a word of the conversation being conducted in the office, and didn't expect to; without doubt it was the kind of conversation which called for undertones.

He took swift note of the fact that the handsome carabiniere was not on duty, and embarked in his excruciating German on the story of the missing camera; it was, as he'd hoped, a subject of negative interest to the officer behind the desk.

After some considerable time, and many misunderstandings over the filling in of forms—they were communicating in a mixture of Italian, English and German—Steve was interested to observe that the door of the office was opening. The lieutenant appeared, gesturing Mark Ackland to precede him. He was in his mid-forties, with dark curly hair, cut short and grey at the sides—trim and slim, particularly in comparison with the large Englishman. He was saying, in good English, '. . . need to find the right man. My sergeant here is local, he'll help you.'

Steve observed the bully-boy with interest. Ackland was a type he knew well, having avoided many such on his ascent of the ladder: overbearing both by inclination and by reason of his schooling, wealth, social position. It would be a pleasure to outwit him, but not, he guessed, an easily attainable pleasure.

As the two men went through the door and down the steps Ackland was looking at his watch, saying something about it being too late. The lieutenant seemed to agree, but what he actually said was rendered inaudible by the hapless officer behind the desk asking for a signature; it had sounded like 'in the morning'.

All in all, Steve considered the visit to have been worth paying, if only for these three fragments of information: it was too late; 'You'll need to find the right man'; and, virtually unheard, something which might have concerned the morning. He left the headquarters feeling relatively pleased with himself, and observed that Mark Ackland and the lieutenant were now talking in the stationary police car.

On his way back to the Café Fontana it occurred to him that he might as well check on their own car, parked on the far side of the *piazza* and now partly concealed by a Volkswagen mini-bus. As it came fully into view, Steve nearly stopped dead in his tracks; leaning against it, cleaning his nails with a pocket-knife, was a bored carabiniere. And that put the entire situation into a *very* different perspective. Steve managed to saunter past, glancing neither at the car nor the policeman.

Getting out of Lazzetta by other means and simply abandoning the Fiat in the *piazza* was Kate's idea; the more they thought about it the better they liked it. Their friendly waiter informed them that Franco Guardini ran the only two taxis available. Once there had been many competitors, but with the failing of the waters . . . He gestured.

Afraid that they might have to wend their way all across town, somehow avoiding the main *piazza*, they were relieved to hear that Signor Guardini's garage was in a yard not far from the back of the café; even more relieved, and surprised, to find that the boss was there and that a relatively new BMW was parked in front of his office.

'Ah no, alas,' said Signor Guardini who was small, pasta-plump, and wore very dark glasses. 'The BMW belongs to a customer. I have no taxi available.'

Kate told him that their wish to go to La Spezia was urgent, they would pay double.

He waved a fat hand in the famous Italian gesture which can mean so many things—in this case, 'too much, too much!'—and said that La Spezia was far away, he didn't normally go that far anyway. 'But as the signorina can see, I have no car for her.'

At that moment one of his taxis turned into the yard and came to a stop. A youth got out. Before Kate could open her mouth Signor Guardini said, rather loudly, loudly enough for the youth to hear, 'Ah no, signorina, the old Renault needs new brake-linings, I would not dare send her on so long a journey. In fact, we must start work on her at once. Emilio, get her into the workshop.'

While the youth turned the Renault and drove it into a shed, aligning it with an inspection pit, Kate and Steve exchanged a glance. She tried once more: 'Signor, perhaps you have a friend who would drive us for such good money.'

'I regret, signorina, that there are few reliable cars in Lazzetta, I could not entrust one so beautiful as you to some old wreck.' He thought for a moment; then spread his hands and shook his head. The dark glasses were levelled at them. 'My deepest apologies, I can think of none.'

When they were barely out of earshot Steve said, 'Deepest apologies, my foot! The police got there before we did.'

'You think so?'

'Damn sure of it.'

'That means they want to keep us here.'

'Looks like it. Let's go eat, I'm starving.'

They retraced their steps to the Café Fontana. It was indicative of their changed attitude that they even lied to the waiter, saying they'd changed their minds about a taxi—too expensive. They ordered the pasta of the day and stared at each other. Kate said, 'Steve, they think they've got us trapped.'

'They could be right.'

'Why? We're not guilty of anything.'

'Since when has guilt mattered to the police.'

'Uncle Mark's not *that* powerful.'

'But he's that rich. You have to look at it from their point of view, Uncle and his friend the lieutenant. They don't want us creeping around, spying on them, fouling up whatever Ackland's come here to do. And he's going to do something, Kate, I definitely heard that bit about needing to find the right man, and the sergeant helping him because he's a local. Uncle's here for a reason.'

'Like what?'

'Oh God, who knows? Falsifying evidence, bribing a witness, pushing someone downstairs—your guess is as good as mine. I bet they plan to grab us when it's all over.'

'Which means tomorrow morning.'

'It sounded like that, I wouldn't swear to it. Uncle looked at his watch and said it was too late, and that must've meant today.'

Kate said, 'Well they're not going to grab us because they're not going to get the chance.'

'Good idea. I'll drink to that.'

They finished their wine—half a carafe, clear heads were called for. He added, 'And if they're not going to grab us it looks as though your very first idea was the best one.'

'Blow?'

He nodded. 'In our own car.'

'You said you were against that.'

'I know what I said. They weren't gunning for us then, now they are.'

'But if there's a cop sitting on the car . . .'

'He doesn't,' said Steve, grinning, 'look like a very intelligent cop.' And then, more seriously, and leaning forward to emphasize it: 'Kate, I'm not quite sure you've got this straight. We're talking about taking the law into our own hands—that's always risky . . .'

'We can't just sit here and *give up*!'

'. . . could be dangerous.'

'So what?'

'So I love you, I don't want you getting hurt.'

The tenderness touched her and she took his hand between both hers. 'Know something? I was damn lucky they heaved that poor bloody dog at me. If they hadn't, I'd never have screamed for you, I could have spent *my whole life* without you!'

'That's known as the fickle finger.'

'How do we operate?'

'Hertz gave us two sets of keys for that car, didn't they?'

'Yes. Both in my bag.'

'Give me one.'

No arrangements had been made to relieve the carabiniere detailed to keep watch on the foreigners' rented Fiat. He had now been there three hours and would have gone over to headquarters to complain had it not been for the presence in town of Lieutenant Canetti. Even though he'd just driven off in his own car you could never tell just when he might turn up again unexpectedly. Leaning, as he now was, against the rear window so that he could chat to anyone he knew who happened to pass along the pavement, he was taken by surprise when he heard the sound of a key in a lock just behind him. He wheeled around and saw that the girl had appeared from nowhere and was unlocking the door on the driver's side. She was a pretty girl, so he put on his most winning smile and said, 'This is your car, signorina?'

Kate looked up at him and walked around the car as she replied, 'No, it's rented. From Hertz, you can see the sticker.'

The man shook his head and tut-tutted. 'I don't know why these people always choose Hertz.'

'What people? What are you talking about?'

'I regret, signorina, the car is stolen.'

'But that's nonsense, I can show you the papers.'

The carabiniere was just about to ask her where her gentleman-friend had got to when he appeared from behind the Volkswagen mini-bus. He said in English, 'What's the matter?'

'Oh, some story about the car being stolen. He wants to look at the rental papers.' And to the carabiniere, 'You'll see they're perfectly in order.'

Steve now opened the driver's door and took the documents from the glove compartment; to do this he had to lean right across the interior. He passed them through the passenger door to Kate, and was then very slow about getting out of the car.

The carabiniere took the Hertz folder and said, 'I must ask you both to come with me and make a statement.'

'Oh, what a nuisance!' replied Kate and began to follow him. At the same moment Steve slipped his key into the ignition and the engine sprang to life. The carabiniere wheeled around startled to find the car already moving. Kate gathered all her strength and gave him a mighty push; then jumped for the swinging passenger door which was now abreast of her. By the time the policeman had recovered his balance the little Fiat was accelerating past him across the *piazza*, Kate just slamming the door.

'Jesus,' said Steve, 'it worked!'

Looking over her shoulder as they plunged into the tree-lined boulevard, Kate caught a glimpse of the carabiniere running towards the police station. 'Will they follow?'

'Depends if they've got a car lined up.'

'The lieutenant's had gone.'

'I know. Maybe they'll be delighted to see the back of us—could save them a lot of trouble.'

At the end of the boulevard the town suddenly petered out, as if the drying up of the waters had truncated it: one or two forlorn villas and a cluster of modern housing; then open countryside and a sign pointing down the only road: 'San Pietro Vara, 12 Km. Autostrada (via Sestri) 43 Km.'

The small Fiat could work itself up to a considerable turn of speed, particularly on a downhill run; and after a mile Kate was able to report that there was still no sign of pursuit; nothing seemed to be moving either in or around the little town on the hillside. It began to look as if their plan was not so stupid after all: a change of car and clothing, perhaps some limited form of disguise, and a furtive return to Lazzetta after dark, probably on foot for the last part of the journey; it shouldn't prove impossible to find where Mark Ackland was staying—there was little choice—and to keep an eye on his movements.

Again looking behind them, Kate saw that some kind of vehicle was now leaving the town, but it didn't seem to be in a hurry and could have belonged to any harmless citizen going about his own business. While she was still staring she heard Steve's shocked voice: 'Oh bloody hell!'

She turned and saw what he'd seen. A few hundred yards ahead a stocky van marked 'Carabinieri' was parked half across the road. There was enough room for one car to squeeze past it—slowly. Three policemen were staring towards the approaching Fiat.

Kate said, 'What do we do?'

'Go for it. Nothing else we *can* do if we want to get away.'

'We've *got* to get away.'

'OK, hold on!'

But a double shock was waiting for them. When they were only one hundred yards from the carabinieri, a battered vehicle, some kind of pick-up, swung into view coming directly towards them and also heading for the gap. Since it was old and going uphill Steve put his foot right down, praying that they'd get there first. Kate took a deep breath and held it. The sound of the Fiat's valiant little engine rose to a high-pitched shriek. There now seemed no doubt at all, even if Steve did get there first, that the two vehicles must meet head-on; but at that very moment the driver of the pick-up realized that this maniac wasn't going to stop, wasn't even going to slow down. With admirable lack of Italian machismo he pulled over to his own side of the road.

They caught a confused glimpse of shocked carabinieri, two falling back behind their van, one taking a dive for safety; there was a moment of frantic high-speed chaos as the little car swerved on to the verge in a cloud of dust and flying pebbles, skidded but missed the police van by a few inches, howled past the astounded driver of the pick-up and regained the road with a squeal of tyres.

Steve shouted, 'One of them had a rifle—get down.'

Kate looked back. '*Get down, Kate!*'

The rifle fired. There was a metallic clang. Fired again, and Steve found himself wrestling with the wheel, mounting the stony bank, veering back on to the road, nearly flying off the far side of it into space, and all the time, slowly, slowly, bringing the car to an ungainly, thumping standstill, dust swirling around them. 'Quite a marksman! Hit the rear tyre on my side.'

They sat there glumly, listening to the cicadas, as the police van, equipped with four-wheel drive, followed them down the road and drew up alongside.

'Out!' said the one who'd had to dive for safety, and had gashed his chin in doing so.

Kate and Steve got out. Beyond the three carabinieri the car which she'd seen emerging from Lazzetta was now quite close. The lieutenant was sitting in the front seat next to his driver. He slid out and approached them, introduced himself by name: Canetti, at their service. He was smiling.

Daniel's only thought on getting to the Woolpack was to phone Italy and, since his sister was sure to be elsewhere, leave a message for her at the Hotel Bobbio; but this plan melted away when Tom's father handed him her own message from Lazzetta: meticulously passed on by Françoise and as meticulously transcribed in Mr Duff's neat handwriting. The mention of Edward Camden as third member of the *ménage* was interesting but not at the moment vital; the news that Mark Ackland had arrived and was in cahoots with the carabinieri didn't surprise Daniel overmuch; but the undoubted fact that this could put his sister in danger, even grave danger, electrified him to further action.

As he was clambering back into the Land-Rover he paused for a moment, frowning at Tom in the driver's seat. Tom, aware of the frown, said, 'What's up? I thought we were in a hurry.'

'By God, I certainly take you for granted, don't I?'

'Well, you can't drive yourself, your little car went up in smoke.'

'That's not the point.'

Tom smiled, leaned over and grabbed his arm, pulling him into the passenger seat. 'If you didn't take me for granted, it wouldn't be much of a friendship, that's what I say.' It was more than he'd ever said before or would ever say again. In spite of the sense of urgency, almost of panic, which gripped him, this unquestioning kindness moved Daniel very much; weary as he now was, he even felt the prick of tears behind his eyes, and turned away swiftly.

'So what next?' demanded Tom.

Daniel sat in silence for a long moment; then: 'Dr Ramsay at the Health Centre.'

'You don't sound too sure.'

Daniel was very far from sure. He had been Angus Ramsay's patient ever since his last, and he hoped final, discharge from hospital; there was little about Daniel's pain, occasional despair, his frustrated hopes of a career and even of marriage which Dr Ramsay did not know all about. He also knew how much Daniel loved his sister and depended on her; indeed he himself had been visibly bowled over by Kate at their only meeting—he was unmarried, not yet thirty. Daniel liked him very much and trusted him, and in that trust lay the uncertainty, for Angus Ramsay was a conscientious doctor with the steel of a strict Scottish upbringing in his soul: not the kind of steel which could easily be bent: yet, Daniel explained to Tom as they drove the six miles into town, if he failed to bend it a disastrous, perhaps fatal, loss of time would ensue; he didn't know where else to go.

Characteristically, Dr Ramsay was in his office, even though afternoon consultations were not due to begin for another half-hour. He was a stocky young man with black hair and black eyebrows which almost met above the bridge of his nose; the dark blue eyes were very direct, honest. So were his words: 'Oh, come on, Dan, you *know* your uncle and his family are registered with me, why the play acting?' The 'play acting' had been intended as a gentle prelude to the critical, the paramount question. This raised the dark brows, but he turned without argument to his files, took out a lean specimen and opened it; then shook his head firmly. Daniel, primed by preconception, said, 'I was afraid you'd give me that.'

'Give you what?'

'Hippocratic Oath, secrets of the consulting room, et cetera.'

Angus Ramsay's smile lightened the incipient heaviness of his features and made him look boyish. 'What a one for jumping to conclusions! The fact is, your grand relatives don't stoop to wee doctors like me. I've only ever clapped eyes on them twice when one of the girls had bronchitis. Result—I have no particulars—not a one.' And he thrust the file under Daniel's nose.

It was true. The two visits were noted, but height, weight, blood pressure . . . all the usual specifications were blank for every member of the family.

'We have,' added Dr Ramsay, 'our own man in Harley Street. I'm pretty damn sure he's some kind of kin to your auntie; how's that?'

'Lousy,' replied Daniel, heart in stomach. And as for testing the steel in the damned Scottish conscience! He managed to evade rigorous questions about his own state of health, which did not at this moment bear examination, and rejoined Tom in the Land-Rover.

There was no need for Tom to make any inquiries; for the second time that day his friend's face told him everything. Eventually he dared say, 'This is pretty important, right?'

'It's vital, Tom. *Vital.*'

They sat side by side in silence. A blackbird sang and sang from the top of a sycamore. The church clock chimed the half-hour. A distant wailing defined itself as an approaching ambulance; it roared past them on its way to the hospital. Tom, staring after it, said, 'Hey, wait a minute! What about that time he got thrown?'

'Uncle Mark? When?'

'Must've been . . . about a year before you came to live at Woodman's.'

Daniel grimaced to himself; he'd been undergoing the last of his many operations. 'So what about it?'

'Nasty fall. His horse slipped on ice, and he got cut up—

badly. They rushed him off to Oxenham, had to give him a transfusion.'

'Transfusion! Are you sure?'

''Course I'm sure, village talked of nothing else for a week!'

Why Oxenham, thirty miles away in another county? The question streaked across Daniel's mind like a fiery comet. The local hospital, just around the corner, could have dealt with the matter just as efficiently. His heart was pounding; he *knew* he was on the right track. But how could he find his way along it? There was only one answer swift enough to make any sense, and it meant that now he *would* have to get to grips with that strict Scottish upbringing—Hippocratic Oath included. There was a single glimmer of hope; it lay in the slight note of bitterness which had crept into Angus Ramsay's voice when he'd said, 'The fact is, your grand relatives don't stoop to wee doctors like me . . . We have our own man in Harley Street.' Daniel recalled that the strict upbringing had also been an uncompromisingly Socialist one. Unfair advantage? Perhaps, but the only tool to hand, and he intended to make full use of it.

Dr Ramsay, who was expecting his first patient in ten minutes, listened silently to Daniel's request, dark brows meeting in disapproval.

Daniel added, 'I can hardly go over to Oxenham and ask questions myself, they'd throw me out.'

'Ay, they would.'

'But if another doctor, the Acklands' own doctor, asked them . . .'

Up came the direct blue eyes. 'Why do you want to know, Daniel?'

'If I were to say Uncle Mark fell off a horse in Italy, needs another transfusion, and has forgotten his . . .'

'*I'd* throw you out.'

Daniel nodded. 'So I'm going to tell you the truth, Angus.

Nobody else knows, and the only reason I dare trust you is because your bloody integrity will make you keep it to yourself.'

'But it may not make me ring the hospital on your behalf.'

Daniel hoped it wasn't just his imagination which caught a glimpse of the good doctor and the good Socialist facing each other behind those honest eyes. He said, 'It may not, but something tells me it will.'

Tom saw the smile on Daniel's face as soon as he came out of the Health Centre. 'Got it then?'

'I certainly did. Ramsay even had a friendly colleague over at Oxenham—never mentioned it to me, of course. By God, they're a canny lot!'

'And?'

'Uncle Mark's O-Positive, Tom. How's that for a blood group?'

'Fine by me if it's fine by you.'

'Putting it mildly. I need a telephone.'

'Public?'

'Private, very private.' He glanced at his watch and was both pleased and surprised to see that their hyperactive and seemingly endless day had not yet reached five-thirty. All the same, this meant that he must make at least one short call from a public phone if he was to stand a chance of catching Peter Henchman before he left his office. Henchman was the closest of his friends from law school, now a junior partner in the family's high-powered practice. What Daniel told him was startling enough to make him cancel a dinner-party and stay at Lincoln's Inn until he received another call; he would even phone his father and ask him to come back to the office right away. Henchman, Clyde & Henchman had learned, in the course of a couple of centuries, how to recognize a potentially lucrative emergency when they encountered one.

By the time Tom and Daniel had got back to the Woolpack, and Daniel had spent a further hour and a quarter talking to the Henchmans, father and son, he was beginning to tremble with fatigue. When the Duff family heard that he proposed to catch an eleven p.m. flight from Heathrow that same night, they at first tried dissuasion, and, that failing, took his welfare into their own capable hands. Mrs Duff left her husband to cope with the bars and cooked a sturdy meal of local cured ham and eggs from her own yard; meanwhile Tom, overriding complaint as he had on the night of Daniel's bloodstained arrival in the wheelchair, took him to the bathroom, washed him all over and dressed him in clean clothes, hissing and humming throughout as if his crippled friend were a nervous horse.

Once again Daniel bit back his dislike of being manhandled; he knew he couldn't have managed by himself, and knew that he was going to need every ounce of his failing stamina to survive what lay ahead.

All police stations possess certain common denominators. No matter that this one was finished with many a *fin-de-siècle* embellishment, there was still the unmistakable smell of armpit, dust, disinfectant overlying urine. Lieutenant Canetti appeared in the doorway of the reasonably clean but shabby cell, labelled 'Waiting-Room', into which Kate and Steve had been thrust. Looking more than ever like a sleek and contented cat, he said, 'You're very foolish. It was merely necessary for you to answer certain questions concerning your car, which is thought to have been stolen. Now you have refused to cooperate with the carabinieri and have damaged the car in question while trying to make a suspicious escape. These are illegal offences to which dangerous driving will be added. Charges will be made.'

'OK,' said Steve, 'let's get on with it.'

'The exact nature of the charges will be decided by the

visiting magistrate who comes to Lazzetta once a week on Fridays.'

'But,' cried Kate, 'that's the day after tomorrow.'

'Precisely.'

They had agreed, on the drive back into town, to make no reference to Mark Ackland, but it was difficult to refrain from doing so now—in no uncertain terms. Perhaps the lieutenant had taken note of their diplomatic omission; he gave a thin smile. 'The sergeant in charge here will attend to your case. You'll be given access to a lawyer should that prove necessary.' The door shut and they were left on their own.

Steve grimaced. 'Looks a bit like game, set and match to Uncle Mark.'

'No, *never*! Something'll happen.'

'It'd better be a miracle. This'll teach you not to go asking me to help you.'

Kate smiled, went over to him and kissed him. 'Make a good story to tell the children—how Mummy and Daddy went to prison.'

'Children, eh? How many do you have in mind?'

'How about . . . one point five like the Chinese?'

'Better make it two. Point five would look silly on a bicycle.'

Kate laughed. 'This is *serious*, we shouldn't be making jokes.'

'Children are no joke. But it's the only way to stay sane in clink.'

She looked at him closely. 'You're speaking from experience, aren't you? You never told me you'd been inside.'

'Not properly, I was only a kid. I was a bit of a tearaway until they channelled my energy into stark ambition. I'm not exactly proud of it.'

Kate stood up and paced about the dismal room. 'Do you suppose we could just walk out? The door's not locked.'

'I think we're in enough trouble as it is.'

'Perhaps we should demand to speak to the British Consul—that's what they always do in books.'

'When the writer wants an easy excuse. Have you ever *tried* calling a Consul, it's worse than British Rail.'

She sighed and sat down again, close to him. 'You're the expert—what happens next?'

He smoothed back her glossy hair and kissed her lightly. 'The bad part happens next, love. They give us some food, then they separate us and stick us in different cells for the night.'

She stared at him, not having thought of this, but of course he was right. After the food, more pasta of the day brought over from the Café Fontana, there appeared the carabiniere whom they'd tricked in the *piazza*; he was looking properly truculent and jangling keys, which clearly gave him pleasure.

Ignoring him, Steve took Kate in his arms and held her tightly. 'Don't let it get you down—that's the idea of it. Try to sleep. It isn't easy but it's the best way out.'

They were led down a gloomy corridor, and he was locked into the first cell they came to. The carabiniere jerked his head, and Kate followed him. Just as they were rounding the corner at the end of the corridor, Steve's voice, evidently speaking through the iron flap on the door, called out, 'Remember, there's going to be a miracle.'

'I'll remember.'

The carabiniere handed her over to an embarrassed-looking woman who might have been someone's aunt dragged unwillingly from her own hearth. She ushered Kate into another cell: a bed, a blanket and a hard pillow, a pot in the corner, a barred window high in the wall.

Kate wandered to and fro for a while; inspected the bed which, like the rest of the cell, seemed fairly clean. Finally, wishing she was wearing jeans rather than the dress she'd put on that morning for the contessa's benefit (it seemed a week ago), she lay down. It was too early for sleep, so she listened to the sparse sounds of ordinary life which came in through the high window. Presently the standard fears and despondencies known to anyone who has ever been incarcerated, even for a few hours, came creeping out of the corners of the ugly little room to taunt her. She found that if she thought, with concentration, about her uncle and his high-handed behaviour she could induce anger, and that anger fought fear and despondency to a standstill.

Steve did not expect his previous experience of being locked up to come to his aid. Cell-fever was such a well-known complaint that it should long ago, he thought, have lost its evil power; but it had not, and perhaps it never would, because it ran counter to the whole of human nature. Finally he began to rehearse in his mind everything he intended to say to Guido Amari when he reached the office in Turin; and presently, for it was an extremely boring conversation, and the day had been long, eventful and tiring, he fell asleep out of sheer exhaustion.

Kate dozed fitfully, forever caught between the unreal world of wakefulness and the equally unreal world of dreams. She might have denied that she'd ever slept at all had she not woken with a start to find sunlight slanting into the cell. It was nearly 7.30. Presumably the carabinieri were content to let their prisoners sleep all day, thus eliminating the need for further invented illegalities.

After a moment she became aware of what had woken her: a deep Italian male voice holding forth *fortissimo* in the distance. She could only catch a word or two here and there; '. . . are you presuming to tell *me* . . . in the name of God, what's that supposed . . . ? . . . when I say at once I mean at once . . .'

Kate rolled off the bed, running both hands through her hair, and hurried to the door, hoping to hear more clearly.

However, as she approached, it opened in her face. The handsome carabiniere, whom they'd first seen the night before last, stood at attention as if turned to stone; his face was the colour of stone too. 'Signorina—if you please.'

Bewildered, Kate walked past him into the corridor and saw, through the open door at the end of it, like something out of the dream-haunted night, her brother, Daniel. He was standing in the entrance-hall looking strained and pale. She let out a cry and ran forward, throwing her arms around him and feeling, in the tension of his frail body, and out of the deep knowledge she had of him, how truly exhausted he was. The owner of the *basso profundo*, a large Italian in a dark grey suit, was leaning over the duty desk, his diatribe pinning the sergeant, also whey-faced, to the wall behind it: '. . . national press, no less than your superiors in Rome, will be *fascinated* when I reveal how you conduct yourselves in Lazzetta.'

Now Steve was coming into the room, looking dazed as well he might; was kissing Kate on the cheek while formal introductions wove an inexplicable pattern: 'Steve, this is my brother . . . Peter Henchman, Kate—you've often heard me . . . And this'—the massive Roman—'is Rico Damiani, the most famous . . .'

It was all meaningless, and in any case they were already moving quickly out of the police station, being ushered into a pair of imposing black limousines. Kate had lost Daniel who was being heaved by Damiani into the first of them, which accelerated away across the *piazza*, watched in astonishment by the buyers and sellers at a small market.

Kate stumbled into the second and was relieved to find Steve beside her, an arm around her. Peter Henchman sat opposite them: a smooth, fair young Englishman who, Kate now remembered, had been Daniel's great friend during his interrupted stay at university: the son and grandson of a famous family of lawyers. He was saying, '. . . but thank

God I happened to be in London—Daniel got hold of me right away. And we were lucky to find Rico Damiani so quickly, he's the Italian end of the business. Flew up to Genoa to meet us.'

Throwing them all off-balance, the car swerved on to a stony track; it was a moment before Kate recognized it as the one leading to the cemetery. They stopped abruptly next to the other limousine in a whirlwind of flying dust, out of which emerged a strange tableau. Daniel was standing at the edge of the terrace facing Mark Ackland whose face was a red mask of rage. As she and Steve reached their level, Kate saw that the grave of Edward Lifford Camden lay between them. The simple headstone had toppled backwards and the coffin was now visible between piles of earth, obviously just uncovered by two workmen who stood by, open-mouthed.

Their uncle advanced on Daniel, lurching, but the massive Italian lawyer took a step forward and thrust him aside as if he were a child; then snapped an order to Lieutenant Canetti of the carabinieri who jumped to obey, blank with shock. He took his erstwhile colleague in the standard armlock and jerked him backwards.

Unable to free himself, Ackland shouted, 'This is a farce. Edward Camden's family want him re-buried in English soil, and I agreed to undertake . . .'

Daniel, hair on end, teetering over the grave on his crutches, shouted back, 'Bullshit! You *are* Edward Camden!'

CHAPTER 13

On the evening of the following day, Kate and Daniel and Steve sat on a hillside terrace above the forested coast which lies south and east of Sestri Levante. The sun, like a huge blood-orange, was falling visibly towards its nightly drowning in the Mediterranean, but on this particular evening the glitter was not blinding, merely magical. The restaurant had been recommended to them by Rico Damiani, the Italian lawyer, whose size alone demonstrated his expertise in such matters. In fact, the Hotel Francesca, to which it belonged, was still closed until the start of the summer season, but a telephone call from the *maestro* had opened its doors for the three of them, and had summoned up what was to prove a memorable meal. Its fragrance occasionally wafted towards them as they sipped their apéritifs.

They had all but recovered from the events of the past three days, including endless, and endlessly repetitive, questioning, in Italian and English, from an assortment of policemen and lawyers. They had slept. They could now, with a continuing sense of surprise, piece together the strange story in which they had played integrated but disparate parts.

Daniel said, 'I can't understand how I was so dumb. Time and again I had it all, and I couldn't see it for looking.'

Steve gestured with his glass. 'But you didn't have it all, did you? Kate had parts and you had parts, but you were in different countries, you couldn't put them together.'

As if still unconvinced, Kate said, 'I suppose it *was* Helen's doing, it had to be.'

'No doubt of that.' Daniel was positive.

'My God, I never liked Auntie but you've got to hand it to her. Such an incredible . . . *daring* plan, and she nearly got away with it.'

'Would have done if it hadn't been for that useless shelf in my little cottage.' He banged a fist on the table. 'But Rosemary Howard told me Helen was the prime mover and I never picked it up.' He recounted the old woman's words at their second meeting: how their grandmother had said that it was all Helen's fault, that she 'had only married Mark for the money, because he was the heir to Longwater, and come hell or high water that was what she intended to get'. He groaned at the memory. 'And do you know what I said? I said, "But Helen had already *got* Longwater years before." I missed it completely—just as I missed the point of what Grandmother said about Mark staying away too long, never coming back to see her.'

'But she was the one who threw him out of England.'

'Yes, we talked about that too. Rosemary told her to her face—she didn't want him to come and visit her, wouldn't have spoken to him if he had.'

'Absolutely right,' said Kate. Then, catching her breath: 'Oh, I see. Grandmother meant that if she'd seen him once or twice in all that time . . .'

'Sixteen years.'

'. . . she'd have noticed that things weren't kosher—she'd have realized pretty quickly, this wasn't her son.'

'Exactly. Whereas after sixteen years you'd naturally expect big changes. And by then their relationship was non-existent anyway, they were barely speaking to each other. That's why she took so long to tumble to it.'

'I wonder how she tumbled in the long run?'

'Maybe,' observed Steve, 'an outside person, like this Rosemary, made some comment and set her thinking. Or the phoney Mark himself could have slipped up without knowing it. He was walking a tightrope, wasn't he?'

'Could've been instinct,' added Kate. 'There's always a deep thing between mothers and sons—perhaps she just ... felt it.'

The three of them brooded on this question, to which they'd never know the answer. They refilled their glasses from bottles which the waiter had left on the table—it was that sort of restaurant.

Eventually Kate asked, 'When do you suppose the idea actually came to Helen?'

Steve thought it must have been when she realized that Edward Camden was genuinely in love with her, genuinely hooked.

'Are women ever that sure?'

'Aren't they?' He grinned. 'Aren't you? I'm hooked.'

'According to Rosemary,' said Daniel, 'Mark and Helen were the toast of the town when they first went to Europe— top of everyone's list. Then Mark began to go too far. His naughty little pranks began getting on people's nerves, and pretty soon they were getting the universal cold shoulder. Nobody wanted to know.'

Steve nodded. 'Let's say it was sometime around then that they met Camden. He and Helen started their love affair. I wonder if Mark minded.'

Kate thought he was probably too far gone. 'Falling in and out of every kind of bed. I bet Helen refused to sleep with him. I'd have refused.'

'Did your Dr Montieri think he was ill by then?' asked Daniel. 'Before Tangier?'

'He couldn't know. But he was sure that Tangier finished him off. That was really the beginning of the end.'

'He must have been pretty far gone before she put her plan to Camden.'

'By God!' Steve laughed. 'I bet it floored him. Can you imagine it? I'd have run a mile.'

'But he wasn't you, my love. As far as the lawyers can

make out he was a good-looking, well-educated, penniless bum. No family in England, only a much-divorced mother last heard of in California.'

'Do bums go to Eton?'

'By the dozen,' replied Daniel. 'And that would have been a big bond between him and Uncle Mark—both Etonians—they were the same kind of man.'

'And looked a bit the same too,' said Kate. 'Enough the same anyway. I wonder if that's why Helen chose him.'

'Highly likely. Anyway she put it to Camden, and Camden wasn't me, he didn't run a mile, he agreed.'

Kate smiled. 'You might have agreed too, in your younger days. From penniless bum to Lord of the Manor of Longwater, one of the richest men in England.'

Daniel shook his head disbelievingly. 'But *how* did she do it, Kate? Did your people in Lazzetta give you any clues?'

'Reading between their lines, yes. She played a waiting-game. Nobody was speaking to them any more, they'd been travelling around *à trois* for over a year. The contessa said they landed up in Verona. Fair enough. While they were there, Helen rented the villa above Lazzetta and waited until Mark was obviously dying. That was the vital turning-point, the . . . what's the word?'

'Crux,' supplied Daniel.

'It called for exact timing.'

'And,' added Steve, 'nerves of steel.'

'When they left Verona she had a mortally sick husband and a healthy lover. When they got to Lazzetta she had a mortally sick lover and a healthy husband. Everyone fell for it, even Dr Montieri.'

'Everyone,' Steve pointed out, 'except a certain lieutenant of the carabinieri.'

'He was a sergeant then.'

Daniel shook his head. 'I missed some of that. The flight

suddenly came up and hit me, I thought I was going to pass out.'

Kate laid her hand over his and held it while Steve elaborated. 'I can't help feeling sorry for Canetti: he had an ambitious wife and too many children. Of course, it was his duty as chief in Lazzetta to ask for the dead man's passport.'

'We know they were quite alike,' observed Daniel. 'I wonder if he noticed the difference right away.'

'I wonder too. By Mediterranean standards they were just two large fair Englishmen, both with moustaches.'

Kate said, 'Do you think Camden always had a moustache, or did Helen make him grown one to look more like Uncle Mark?'

'Sounds her style—attention to detail.' Steve shrugged and continued: 'So Canetti had this large family. And policemen are notoriously underpaid. I bet he'd spent years keeping an eye open for the main chance. Don't we all? I know I did until my luck changed. This was his main chance and he grabbed it with both hands.'

'So they had to bribe him.'

'What else? They had no alternative. And remember, Camden was soon going to acquire Ackland money. He and Canetti must have made a long-term deal—further regular payments in exchange for a continued safeguarding of the situation.'

'Very Italian,' said Kate. 'They've been at it for thousands of years.'

Steve smiled. 'Very human, regardless of nationality.'

'Complicated, though.'

'No, love, not at all, Canetti just made sure, when he left Lazzetta for higher things in Sestri or wherever, that one of the lads was paid a small retainer to watch the pot. And after a while what shows up?'

'Me. *Not* minding my own business.'

'Correct. Promptly reported to Lieutenant Canetti who promptly reports to so-called Uncle Mark.'

'You've jumped ahead,' said Daniel. 'You know what went on in Lazzetta, I don't.'

'Where were we?'

'Mark Ackland died and was buried. What next?'

Kate took up the story, obliquely recounted to her by the contessa and Dr Montieri. 'As soon as she could decently do so, Helen put more space between herself and events—moved her new husband on to La Spezia.'

'Where,' said Steve, 'our luscious friend Julia suspected a thing or two but couldn't put her finger on specifics.'

'She didn't get much time, did she?'

Daniel glanced at his sister. 'Corsica right away?'

'Pretty well, yes. And in Corsica they stayed. That must have driven Helen bananas. All she wanted was to be Queen of Longwater, but she had to stick it out in Cortiano as a farmer's wife. Have children. Let Edward Camden grow into the skin of Mark Ackland—a middle-aged Mark Ackland.'

Steve shook his head in unwilling admiration. 'The waiting-game. What a woman! How old was she then?'

'When they arrived in Corsica? She wasn't even thirty.'

'A bit young for exile.'

'She paid a few visits to England.' Kate could dimly remember some of those visits: awkward glimpses of childhood when she and Daniel were staying with their grandparents at Longwater: the 'foreign' cousins. They came with their mother, only with their mother. The story obviously was that Mark, still smarting from the way old Lydia had treated him, refused to meet her. This antagonism would carry over nicely when he finally reached England; by then the gulf between mother and son was too wide to bridge; they seldom even tried. No doubt Helen nurtured the seeds of estrangement with care and cunning.

'How long *were* they in Corsica?' asked Daniel.

'Eight years.'

'Are you sure?'

'Yes. I met a lovely woman called Gianetta who'd been nurse to all the children. She was a bit puzzled by the eight years too. She said, "It was as if they were hiding from something or somebody." Pretty acute! She thought Mark, as I suppose we must call him, had done something wicked in the past.'

'He had.'

'Sure. But that wasn't what they were hiding from. They just knew that transition takes time. He aged. He produced three children. He put on weight. He became a respected tenant and farmer. If anyone in England knew or cared they probably said, "I hear Mark Ackland's grown up. At last!"'

'By God,' said Steve, 'it must have been a stomach-churning moment when Helen decided the waiting-game was over—when they finally went back to Longwater.'

Daniel wasn't so sure. 'Sixteen years is a hell of a long time. Mark's old friends would have changed as much as he had. Anyway they were scattered all over the place—none of them had clapped eyes on him for at least a decade. And most important of all, Lydia was nearly blind, didn't want to have anything to do with her elder son, and had retired to Woodman's.'

'Why did she do that?'

'You don't imagine,' said Kate, 'she'd have shared the big house, *her* house, with those two? Never in a thousand years. And by then her sight had almost gone, she was happier in a confined space.'

'All the same, that first meeting with her must have scared Camden witless.'

'Probably. But Helen was there to stage-manage. Knowing Grandmother, she probably spent the whole time telling him how much she missed his brother—our dad. And anyway, Steve, it was all worthwhile, it worked. He took over the place and made a good job of it. The county must have been thunderstruck.'

'And Helen finally got everything she wanted.'

'Did she ever!' Kate laughed softly. 'In a couple of ticks she'd established herself as the richest and most influential woman in the southern counties. And the most brilliant hostess—her houseparties even hit the headlines. And it went on for years, they must have thought they were as secure as the Bank of England.'

Daniel grimaced. 'Let's say the Bank of Geneva.'

'Good point. And then . . . then Grandmother had her little moment of inspiration. We'll never know what brought it on, and it doesn't much matter. She just *knew*, without a shadow of doubt, that the man lording it over Longwater wasn't her son. She summoned her best friend, poor old Rosemary. Right, Daniel?'

'Yes. And drove her up the wall by telling her half-truths she couldn't properly understand . . .'

'Grandmother all over. She couldn't bring herself to really *trust* anyone, not one hundred per cent.'

'Rosemary was afraid she'd flipped and was going to land herself in all kinds of legal trouble. That's why she advised her to consult her lovely son, Andrew the lawyer. Big mistake! Lydia was always a sharp judge of character, she didn't trust him and she was dead right. But by then she must have said a little too much. Andrew popped over to Longwater, currying favour or even with an eye on future blackmail, and told Helen and the man who wasn't our Uncle Mark that the old lady was going to cause big, big trouble. *He* didn't know what he was talking about but they damn well did.'

'What a moment!' Kate shook her head. 'Macbeth and The Wife weren't in it!'

' "But screw your courage to the sticking-place, and we'll *not* fail." Edward Camden did just that. I suppose he asked for a private interview—probably suggested Sally should be sent out for a while in case of eavesdropping.'

Steve said, 'I wonder she wasn't scared, I wonder she let the girl go.'

'Grandmother scared! That would have been the day. And she never, but never, discussed family matters if any stranger might overhear. Go on, Daniel.'

'Well, we can only guess. I suppose Grandmother told him she knew he was an impostor and could prove it.'

'I wonder if Auntie Helen was there too.'

'Could've been. Anyway there was no choice of options, was there? Camden got hold of that spare newel-post and killed her with it. Accident. Blind old lady falls downstairs when faithful companion is absent and hits her head on identical newel-post.'

'And,' said Steve, 'it worked.'

'Yes—reprieved. They were probably feeling nicely relaxed again by the time two young carpenters fished Rosemary's letter out from behind the panelling in my kitchen. And Kate took off.'

'We both took off.'

'I was a slow starter, I was chicken. But Kate, do you realize the whole thing was there in that letter, staring us in the face from the word go? She wrote how sorry she was she'd lost her temper when Lydia mentioned the Ackland blood. Rosemary thought she was being a boring old snob, but that wasn't what she meant at all, she was just being practical.'

'And the blood thing,' asked Steve, 'it's conclusive evidence?'

'Absolutely. A-Negative is quite a rare group. Grandfather Ackland and both his sons belonged to it, and so do I. Uncle Mark's medical records in several countries will list A-Negative. Edward Camden's O-Positive.'

'Even Helen,' added Kate, 'couldn't change that.'

'They didn't intend to use any local doctors. And their man in Harley Street knew nothing about other members of the Ackland family, so why would Helen care about blood groups, who was going to ask?'

'*You* asked.'

'Only because we were already on to them. Good thing Tom remembered he'd had a riding accident—good thing Angus Ramsay followed it up for me.'

'Must've shocked him rigid.'

'It did, or he'd never have called Oxenham and I'd have been up the creek without a paddle.'

'Anyway,' said Steve, 'some surgeon in Venice gave you the clincher. How did Uncle fall out of that window, do we know?'

'Probably pissed. Or stoned.'

'Or pushed,' suggested his sister, unconsciously echoing Rosemary Howard. 'I bet a lot of people wouldn't have minded pushing him by then.'

Daniel gave a small sigh of satisfaction. 'Yes, the metal plate on his leg's the clincher all right. First thing the Coroner saw when they opened the coffin.'

'So your grandmother was right all along the line.'

Kate laughed. 'Of course. She always was—and didn't she let you know it!'

CHAPTER 14

Edward Camden and Lieutenant Canetti had been arrested at once in the cemetery at Lazzetta. It was the first ripple of a devastating wave of litigation which was to sweep across Europe, gathering a flotsam of witnesses and depositing them high and dry at the Old Bailey, part of one of the longest and most sensational criminal cases ever tried there.

Television and the Press had a field-day. Many members of the so-called jet-set had made good use of their designated means of transport and had disappeared to various unfashionable (soon-to-be-fashionable, thanks to them) corners of the globe where they could pass a few months incognito; but enough were gathered together in London to supply an ongoing extravaganza of fame and wealth. In the days of their early married popularity Mark and Helen Ackland had certainly known everybody who was anybody in the world of the beautiful people.

Helen herself put on an extraordinary performance, denying nothing (what could she deny?) and accepting her guilt without any impassioned self-defence but with an icy dignity which dismayed all concerned. She was, *par excellence*, the soap opera villainess whom you love to hate. Many people, to their own surprised distaste, found themselves admiring her. Well, almost. And quite soon the usual lunatic fringe was straggling to and fro outside the Old Bailey, demanding her release, and probably her sanctification.

It soon became evident that she had loved neither Mark Ackland nor his surrogate, and more than once she showed quite shocking scorn for her incredulous and horrified children. The psycho-babblers had a field-day too.

Kate, Daniel and Steve gave their breathtaking evidence with commendable calm. Edward Camden broke down and wept, but nobody was impressed. His mother appeared from California in an alcoholic haze and had to be led from the court. Andrew Howard's garbled defence was heard in stony silence and he was disbarred from future legal practice.

But eventually all the flotsam and all the melodrama were washed away by the inexorable tide of time. Helen Ackland and Edward Camden were both given heavy sentences on a variety of charges but murder was not among them. Although forensic investigation found minute traces of blood on the detached newel-post, despite thorough washing, it was impossible to date them and there was no evidence to connect this blunt instrument with Camden's hand; his counsel deflected the indictment. But legal innocence has never had much to do with innocence as the world understands it, and as far as the world is concerned the suspicion of murder will follow them all their lives.

Daniel Ackland is now an enthusiastic patient of Dr Allard at the Blake Clinic where the cure is already showing guarded signs of success. He plans to sell a part of Longwater's abundant acreage and set up a foundation to help other sufferers from Raynor's Syndrome who cannot, like his old self, afford the treatment.

Kate and Steve opted for marriage because they want children and believe that children want parents, preferably two of them. They spent their honeymoon not far from Bastia in a charming little house discovered by Françoise, and are now looking after Longwater pending the return of the heir. Kate expected it to be too reminiscent of its previous inhabitants and was surprised to find this wasn't so: perhaps because they never had any right to be there in the first place.

Steve has given up his job with Boyd Electronics in order to devote all his time to estate management. To his surprise—and to Kate's amusement, remembering his previous antagonism to any such milieu—he is enjoying the whole experience; and though he describes himself as merely a caretaker it seems likely that Daniel, even if he comes back from the United States completely cured, will welcome the assistance, growing skill and hard-won business acumen of his brother-in-law.

Woodman's stands empty. In the village they say that it's haunted by Lydia Ackland. It would be unlike her not to make her presence felt one way or another.